BUILT
TO
LAST

BUILT
TO
LAST

DAVID MACAULAY

HOUGHTON MIFFLIN BOOKS FOR CHILDREN
Houghton Mifflin Harcourt
Boston New York 2010

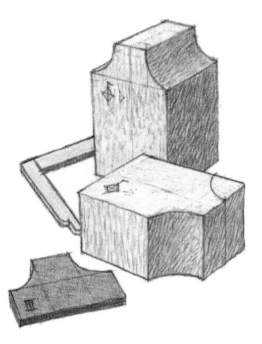

Houghton Mifflin Books for Children is an imprint of
Houghton Mifflin Harcourt Publishing Company.

www.hmhbooks.com

The text of this book is set in Times New Roman and Berkeley Oldstyle.

The line work in this book was drawn with a fountain pen, colored pencil, or regular pencil. The color was created using felt-tip markers, colored pencils, and some watercolor (in *Mosque*). All of the illustrations for *Castle* and *Cathedral* were finished digitally.

The Library of Congress cataloging-in-publication data is on file.

ISBN 978-0-547-34240-5

Manufactured in the United States of America
DOW 10 9 8 7 6 5 4 3 2 1

4500242813

For Julia and Sander

CONTENTS

INTRODUCTION

In the beginning of 2009, I was asked how I would feel about reissuing some of my old architecture books along with *Mosque* in a single volume that, coincidentally, was to be the same size as *The Way Things Work* and *The Way We Work*. The new compendium would be called *Built to Last,* a title I found both interesting and, given the "disposable" times we live in, ironic. My only obligation would be to write an introduction (and probably not this one!). An editor and designer assigned to the project would do the rest, including digitally coloring the old black-and-white material to freshen it up and make it more consistent with the full-color illustrations in *Mosque.* They had me until "colorizing."

Cross hatching—inking layers of lines at different angles to describe form and space through shadow and texture—is what illustrators do or at least used to do when color wasn't available, and my old books are full of it. Putting color either over or under cross hatching after the fact, either to modernize it or make it look like something new, generally results in printed mud. While my protective antennae were chanting "run, don't walk," curiosity had wedged its oversize foot in the doorway. What would *Cathedral* and *Castle* look like in color?

Rather than simply coloring in the old art, I decided to trace it and in the process eliminate all that pesky line work before adding color. After looking at a couple of samples, we all agreed this approach could work and sat down to map out a schedule. The one thing we'd forgotten, especially me, is that time runs in two directions. The art for *Cathedral,* my very first book, was completed thirty-seven years ago, and for *Castle,* four years later. I've spent most of the time between then and now not only making different kinds of books but also teaching illustration, and both have meant continually learning and relearning what it means to communicate through pictures. As a result, while I remain nostalgically attached to my early books, I'm not as easy to please as I was back then.

The more time I spent with the original illustrations, the more suspicious I became. Had I simply seduced a reading public with miles of India ink and a need to draw every brick? There was too much dependence on ambiguous cross sections—a language learned while studying architecture but not so helpful in trying to reach a larger public. There were embarrassing lapses in scale and equally embarrassing attempts at drawing human beings. And of course, there were a few inevitable inaccuracies. With deadlines looming, I realized I couldn't just trace the old drawings; I would have to start from scratch. This would mean reconsidering choices of subject matter, altering sequences, and even throwing away some of my old favorites. And because neither pictures nor words are produced in a vacuum, this would also mean looking again at the text to be sure it was accurate and consistent with the new art.

The inevitable moments of doubt about both the effectiveness of the original books and the logic of this new venture were kept in check by two things. First, the ability of my colleagues at Houghton to talk me down from the cliff from time to time, as they patiently threw away schedule after schedule, and second, the fact that I still believe in the content of those old books. They were created not only to show why and how some of the world's best-

known buildings were designed and constructed, but to connect the bricks and mortar with the vision and courage of the builders. Whether motivated by faith or fear, these were people who lived ordinary lives—raised families, needed jobs, developed skills, and had dreams. In short, they were people like us. By showing how they achieved such extraordinary feats, I hoped and still hope to remind today's "builders" of their own potential.

Whether the three building types in this book were built to last or simply to impress, they were certainly constructed with determination and care. And without the lessons they offer, our past would be more remote and therefore less useful as we stumble into an uncertain future. Of course, these structures don't necessarily represent a time we'd want to relive. The cold castle toilet seats and constant warfare of much of the Middle Ages come to mind—although we seem to have made some serious headway on the former. On the other hand there is the inspiring power of soaring space in the great cathedrals, of light passing through walls of glass to color the air and tell a story. And in the solemn simplicity of the mosques, we still find a place of peace and quiet in the heart of even the busiest cities.

While building to last just long enough may more accurately describe the uncertainties and pessimism of our age, the presence of significant and often inspiring architecture can fuel our own creative capabilities while battling the cynicism that threatens to undermine them. Understanding these buildings and the link they provide to people of another time and place should remind us that anything is buildable, whether of stone or ideas. What matters is to build well and to leave something of consequence behind.

CASTLE

CASTLE

INTRODUCTION

In 1272, upon the death of his father, King Henry III, Edward Longhsanks was named King Edward I of England. In addition to having almost twenty children, he spent much of his royal life working to solidify his power throughout Britain. This put him in conflict not only with various barons in his own country but also with many of the natives of both Scotland and Wales. Although he never succeeded in conquering the Scots, his ambitious and imaginative campaign in Wales did manage to subdue large areas of that country.

In 1277 Edward expanded his strategy in Wales from a purely military engagement to the building of a series of English settlements and castles in strategic locations throughout the land. Although a farsighted solution to the problem, it was also very expensive, so whenever possible he encouraged loyal noblemen to undertake, at their own expense, similar building projects that would fit into his master plan.

Both castle and town were intended as tools of conquest, but each had its own distinct function. The castle and the wall surrounding the town were primarily defensive structures. Whatever offensive use these fortifications had stemmed from their placement along important supply and communication routes and to some extent from their intimidating appearance. Their most important function, however, was to protect the new town. Once established and prosperous, these new towns would provide a variety of previously unavailable social and economic opportunities, not only to the English settlers who would occupy them at first, but eventually to the Welsh as well.

Lord Kevin's castle, although imaginary, is based on several castles built to aid in the conquest of Wales between 1277 and 1305. Their planning and construction epitomized more than two centuries of military engineering accomplishments throughout Europe and the Holy Land. The town of Aberwyvern, also imaginary, is based on towns founded in conjunction with castles in Wales during the same twenty-eight-year period.

On March 27, 1283, King Edward I of England named Kevin le Strange to be lord of Aberwyvern—a rich but rebellious area on the west coast of Wales. Although the title was bestowed out of gratitude for loyal service, the accompanying lands were not granted without a more significant royal motive.

Lord Kevin immediately began making preparations to protect his newly acquired land with the building of a new castle and adjacent town. He hired James of Babbington, a former officer of the King's Works and a master engineer, to design both and oversee their construction.

At the suggestion of King Edward and his advisors they planned to select a site near the mouth of the river Wyvern, a vital link between the sea and the mountainous interior.

In mid-April, Master James and his staff set sail for the Welsh coast with an advance party of soldiers, carpenters, and diggers.

After considering several possibilities, Master James chose a high rocky outcrop that extended into the water. This site took advantage of the natural defensive properties of the river and, at the same time, because of its height, assured an unbroken view of the surrounding countryside. The town would occupy the land at the foot of the outcrop and act as a landward barrier. Together, the town and river would create the castle's first ring of defense.

To increase the security of the future castle, a team of diggers was put to work cutting a trench or moat across the landward side of the outcrop. A second team began digging a well on the site itself. The carpenters meanwhile were building temporary housing for Master James and all the workers, as well as barracks for the soldiers. By the time Lord Kevin arrived a few weeks later, a small compound was already standing on the outcrop protected behind a high wooden fence called a palisade. It was in one of these thatched structures that the plans were presented for Lord Kevin's approval.

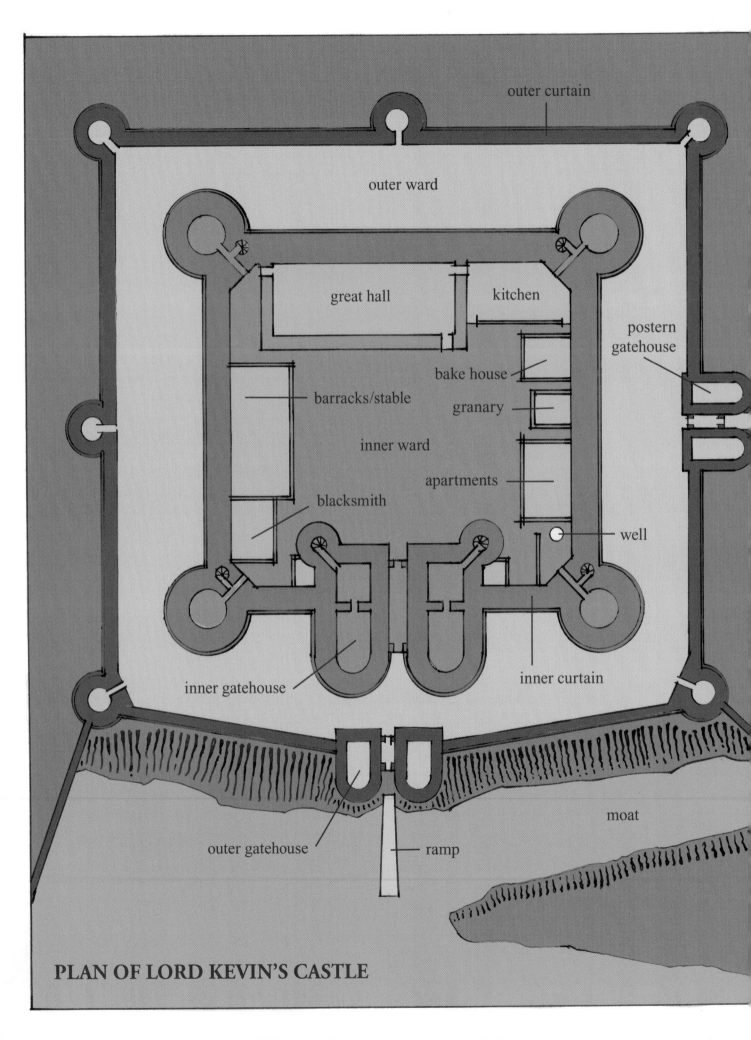

outer curtain

outer ward

great hall

kitchen

postern gatehouse

bake house

barracks/stable

granary

inner ward

apartments

blacksmith

well

inner gatehouse

inner curtain

outer gatehouse

ramp

moat

PLAN OF LORD KEVIN'S CASTLE

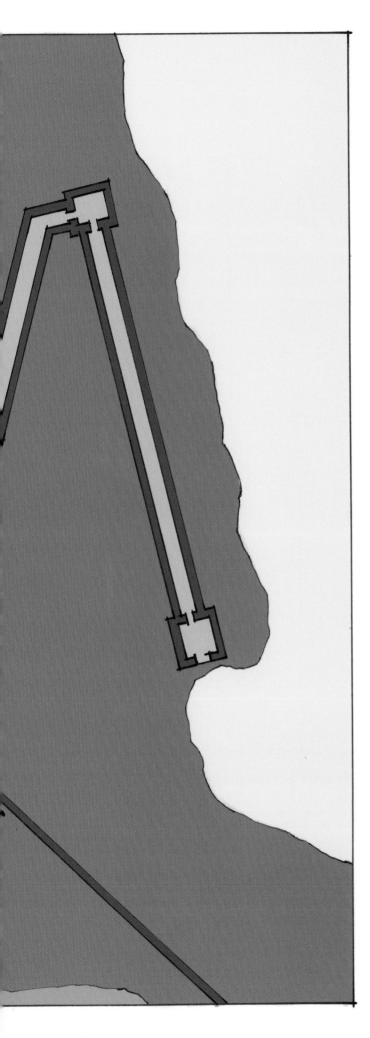

The most important considerations were that both the castle and the town would be able to resist direct attack and withstand a siege. Although quite simple, this last tactic was often very effective and involved surrounding one's enemy and waiting until all food and drink within the walls were gone, leaving the defenders with two equally unpleasant alternatives—starvation or surrender.

In planning the castle defenses, Master James combined several ideas developed in other castles in both Wales and Scotland on which he had served as apprentice to the master engineer. He laid out the castle in a series of progressively smaller yet stronger defensive rings, one inside the other.

At the center of the castle was the inner ward—a large open space enclosed by a wall called the inner curtain. The area surrounding the inner curtain, called the outer ward, was enclosed by a lower wall called the outer curtain. Rounded towers located along both walls made it possible for soldiers to observe the entire perimeter of the structure. The three main entrances were each protected by elaborate and well-fortified gatehouses.

Besides housing Lord Kevin, his family, staff, and servants when they were in Wales, the castle was to be the permanent home of the steward and his family, their staff and servants, and a military garrison. The apartments of both the lord and the steward, along with a chapel, several offices, and a dungeon, were located in the towers of the inner curtain. The rest of the castle's residents lived and worked in buildings in the inner ward.

In planning for the possibility of siege, Master James located the all-important well within the inner ward. This would make it virtually impossible for the enemy to poison the main water supply—an act that would probably ensure the castle's defeat.

watch turret

inner ward

inner curtain

outer ward

batter

The outer curtain, which measured about two hundred feet along each of the four sides, was to be twenty feet high and eight feet thick. The walls of the towers would be of the same thickness, but ten feet higher. The inner curtain measured about one hundred and twenty feet to a side, and was to be thirty-five feet high and twelve feet thick, and its towers would be fifty feet tall. The increased height of the inner curtain would enable soldiers on top of it to fire over and reinforce those soldiers guarding the outer curtain.

Continuous walks along the tops of both curtain walls made it easy for soldiers to get wherever they were most needed during an attack. The wall walk on the outer curtain was reached by staircases located against its inner face. That of the inner curtain was reached by one of the spiral staircases built into the walls. Soldiers on both walks would be protected by a battlement, a narrow crenellated wall of alternating high and low segments built along the outer edge.

Both curtain walls and towers were perfectly vertical, except around the bottom of the outer face, where they angled outward slightly. This sloping base, called a batter, had two main functions. First, it thickened the wall, spreading the great weight over more of the ground, and second, it created a surface off which objects dropped from the tops of the walls would be directed toward the enemy.

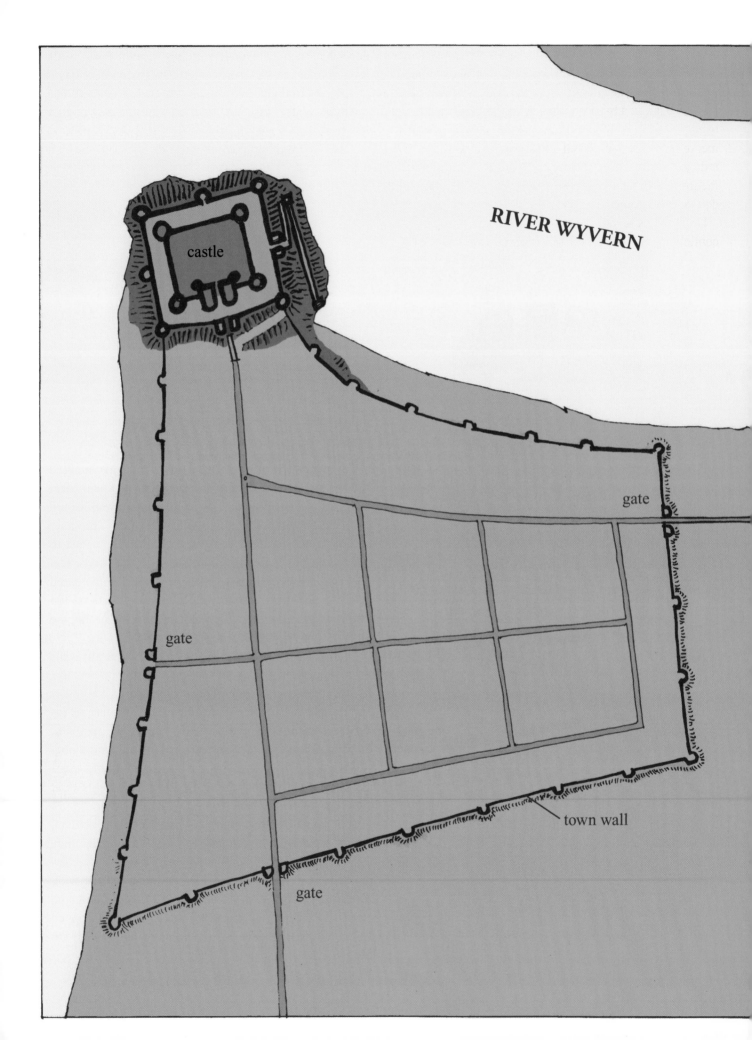

RIVER WYVERN

castle

gate

gate

gate

town wall

In laying out the town, Master James paid particular attention to the arrangement and design of its surrounding wall. Determined entirely by military considerations, this battlemented barrier would be six feet thick and stand twenty feet high. Where it abutted the castle, the battlements would be eliminated and the thickness of the wall reduced to prevent easy access. The three entrances into the town, like those into the castle, were each fortified by double-towered gatehouses.

Unlike the walls of the castle, which were more or less continuous, the town wall was planned as a series of independent sections. Wooden bridges, located at wall-walk level behind each U-shaped tower, were the only means of getting from one section to another. In the event that a portion of the wall was overrun, the defenders simply removed the bridges at each end of that segment, forcing the enemy either to come down the exposed stairway against the inner face of the wall or to go back the way they came.

Lord Kevin immediately instructed his chief clerk, Walter of Boston, to assemble the necessary labor force. Letters were dispatched to the constables of several English cities indicating the numbers and types of workers needed. Since the entire project had the blessing of the king himself, within months more than a thousand men and women were either on hand or on their way. These included more diggers and carpenters, as well as masons, mortar makers, quarrymen, blacksmiths, cart operators, and several hundred basic laborers. Each discipline would

pickax

DIGGERS

pit saw

brace

auger

bit

frame saw

hand saw

CARPENTERS

pickax

crowbar

bean counter

wheel-barrow

measuring stick

QUARRYMEN

MASTER JAMES

be overseen by one or more master craftsmen, who in turn would be responsible to Master James. Housing for the new workers was built at the foot of the outcrop and surrounded by another palisade.

Some workers would arrive with their own tools, but many other tools had to be shipped in. Since most of these were made of iron, they could easily be repaired in one of the blacksmith shops.

blacksmith's hammer

worn-out tools

blacksmith's tongs

BLACKSMITH

lime

water

hoe

sand

MORTAR MAKERS

stonecutter's pickax

hammer and chisel

squares

trowel

level

plumb line

plumb bob

MASONS

Genevieve

Clarisse

CARTMAN

MASTER JAMES'S DOG

Because of the importance of the town, both as a barrier and as a future home to friendly English settlers who would fight to protect what they had been given, it was decided that work should commence simultaneously on the walls of both the castle and the town.

On June 8, 1283, Master James and his surveyors began marking off the placement of all the walls and towers.

Once the perimeter of the town was established, diggers enclosed the entire area with a wide ditch. Along the inside edge of the ditch, carpenters then erected a palisade.

To protect all the workers from Welsh interference, King Edward increased the size of the garrison to one hundred infantrymen, a dozen mounted soldiers, and two dozen crossbow men.

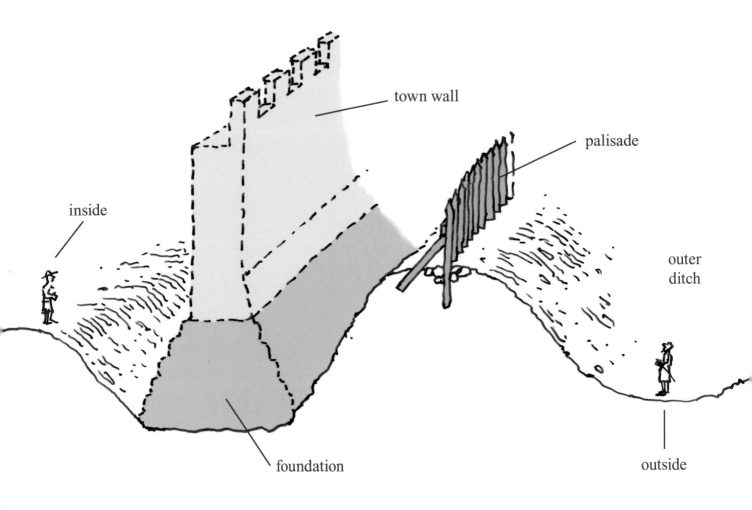

inside

town wall

palisade

outer
ditch

foundation

outside

While large sections of the castle could stand directly on bedrock, much of the town wall would need deep foundations to reduce the chance of uneven settlement and cracking. Several hundred diggers were soon excavating a foundation trench along the inside of the palisade.

In mid-July, the first boatloads of stone and sacks of lime arrived. All the main walls were to be built with an inner and outer face of stone. The mortar used to bind these stones together was made from a precise combination of sand, lime, and water. At intervals of every three or four feet in height, the space between the facing walls was filled with rubble—a mixture of stones and mortar. As the curtain walls continued to grow, masons regularly checked the vertical accuracy of both sides.

Confident that Master James had the project well in hand, Lord Kevin returned to England to see about paying for it. The overall cost was expected to be somewhere around 8,000 pounds, a substantial amount even for a king, never mind a mere lord. Some of the funds would come from rent and taxes to be paid by farmers in the surrounding villages. They automatically became Lord Kevin's tenants when he was given the land on which they lived and worked. To ensure that all due amounts would be collected, the lord's bailiff was dispatched along with a contingent of soldiers to the surrounding countryside to determine the population and record their holdings. The rest of the money would come either from the sale of livestock and produce raised on Kevin's land in both England and Wales or directly from his personal coffers.

By the spring of 1284, the walls had grown high enough for the builders to need a temporary wooden framework called scaffolding. Made of poles lashed together, it was secured to the walls by short horizontal pieces of timber called putlogs. These were set into holes called putlog holes, which had been left in the walls along a gradual incline. Planks were then nailed to the putlogs to create ramps up which the heavy material could be more easily moved.

Work continued until November, when colder temperatures threatened to crack the wet mortar. After protecting the tops of the unfinished walls with a covering of straw and dung, many of the workers returned to England for the rest of the winter. Those that remained worked in the sheds, preparing material and equipment for the resumption of work.

By May of 1285 the curtain walls were rising once again, but still the only towers under construction were those of the all-important gatehouses. Because these were the most vulnerable parts of the castle's defenses, Master James had planned them with great care and all the latest features.

Each gatehouse contained two floors above the entryway. The first was supported on a row of parallel stone arches. The second rested on wooden beams. It was from this, the highest room, that a heavy timber grille called a portcullis could be lowered to block the opening. The portcullis slid up and down in grooves cut into the walls. The bottom of each vertical piece was shaped into a point and like the face of the grille was covered with iron. Beyond the portcullis was a pair of heavy wooden doors, also reinforced with iron. A second pair of doors closed off the rear of the gatehouse. Immediately behind the front doors, two holes faced each other on opposite sides of the passageway. A heavy piece of timber called a drawbar could be slid from one hole and into the other, further securing the doors. Narrow vertical slits called arrow loops were located on both sides of the passage through which a soldier could shoot his arrows and remain completely protected. If unwanted visitors were careless enough to get caught in the space between both sets of doors, they could be fired upon from the sides, while at the same time a variety of missiles could be dropped from openings in the floor above, called murder holes.

In addition to its portcullis and heavy doors, the outer gatehouse also had a drawbridge. This flat timber platform was fastened to the top of an axle, the ends of which were set into holes at the base of each tower. One end of the drawbridge extended toward the castle; the other rested on the end of a narrow twenty-five-foot-high stone ramp that rose from the street below. The castle end of the bridge was weighted, and when the supports were removed it swung down into a specially designed pit cut into the rock between the towers. This made the other end rise, breaking the connection and blocking the entrance. To allow entry, the bridge would then be hoisted back into a horizontal position and the supports replaced.

Anyone wishing to enter the castle would have to climb the ramp and in the process would expose themselves to attack by soldiers along the walls. The postern gatehouse was also finished at this time, and it too would eventually have a drawbridge.

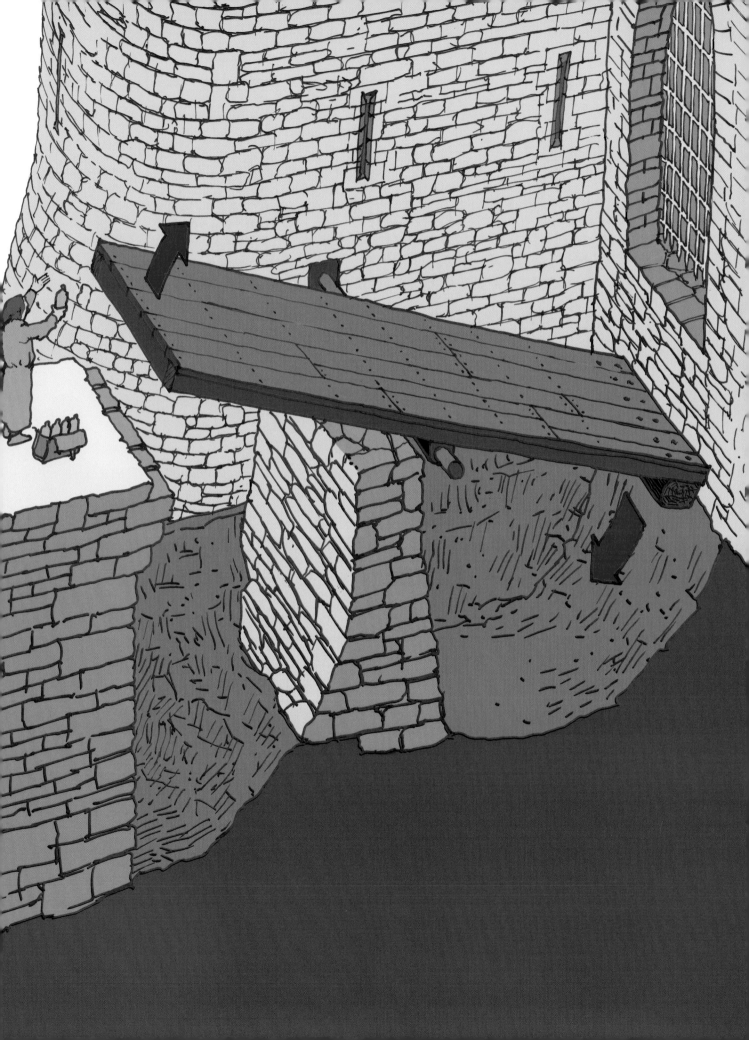

By the end of November the walk along the outer curtain was complete and work had begun on its crenellations. The high segments, called merlons, each contained an arrow loop. The vertical wedge-shaped space behind each arrow loop gave the soldiers more flexibility in aiming their bows. The lower segments, called embrasures, created openings from which a variety of unwelcome items could be dropped on the enemy below.

In order to further intimidate possible attackers, Master James had every merlon capped with vertical stone spikes called finials, making the walls appear even taller and more unassailable than they already were.

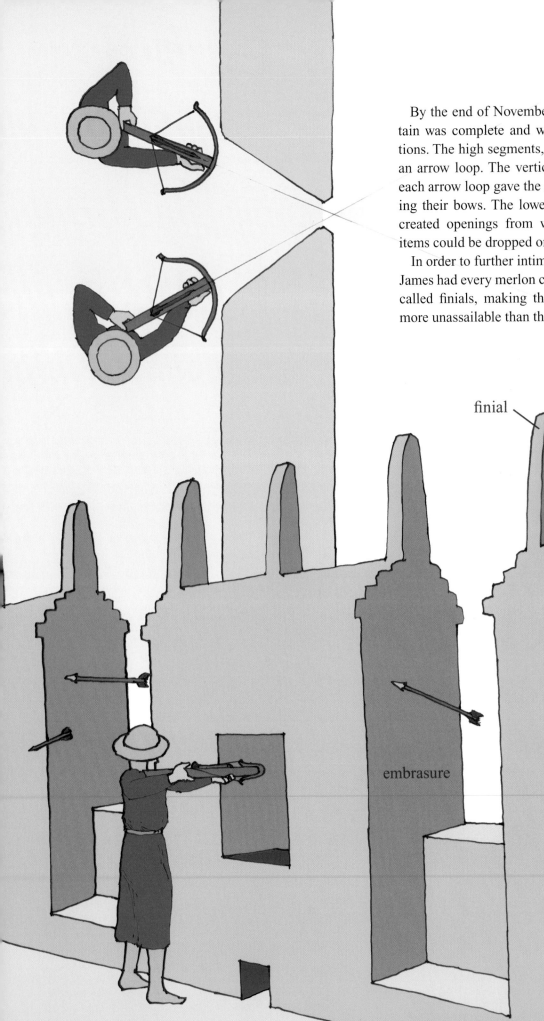

finial

merlon

embrasure

arrow
loop

Throughout the summer and autumn and again the following spring, a workforce of over two thousand toiled away without interruption. In his monthly letter to Lord Kevin in June of 1287, Master James proudly informed his patron that the outer curtain along with its towers was finished and the town wall had reached a height of fifteen feet. He also pointed out that in spite of the possibility of the occasional Welsh attack, a handful of courageous families had already taken up residence along the roads closest to the castle's main entrance. Many of them had come originally to work for Master James or one of his master craftsmen but now had decided to stay and become part of the new town.

In July, at Master James's request, one hundred and fifty
additional masons were hired to speed up work on the inner curtain and its towers.

To increase the defensive strength of the already massive inner curtain, Master James had designed its towers so they could be sealed off and defended independently of the rest of the wall. Each tower had only two entrances, one off the inner ward and one at the level of the wall walk. In the event that the inner ward was ever overrun, both openings could be sealed off by heavy wooden doors.

The towers, including those of the inner gatehouse, would house the castle's most important residents. Each contained a number of floors, connected by spiral staircases built into the thickness of the wall. These staircases continued above the level of the tower walk to the top of the slender watch turret.

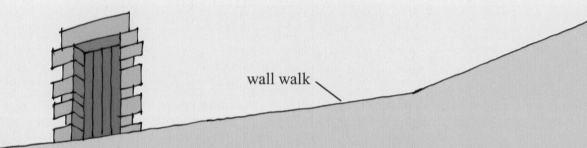

wall walk

The room at ground level, called the basement, was usually used for storage, enabling a tower to be self-sufficient during a siege. The upper rooms were used either as office or living space. All the upper floors were made of wooden planks nailed to heavy oak beams, which spanned the interior of each tower at the required height. The beams were either inserted into the wall or supported by projecting stone blocks called corbels.

In one tower of the inner curtain, Master James took advantage of a depression in the rock below to locate a dungeon. The only entrance was a trapdoor in the basement floor, and there was no need for any light.

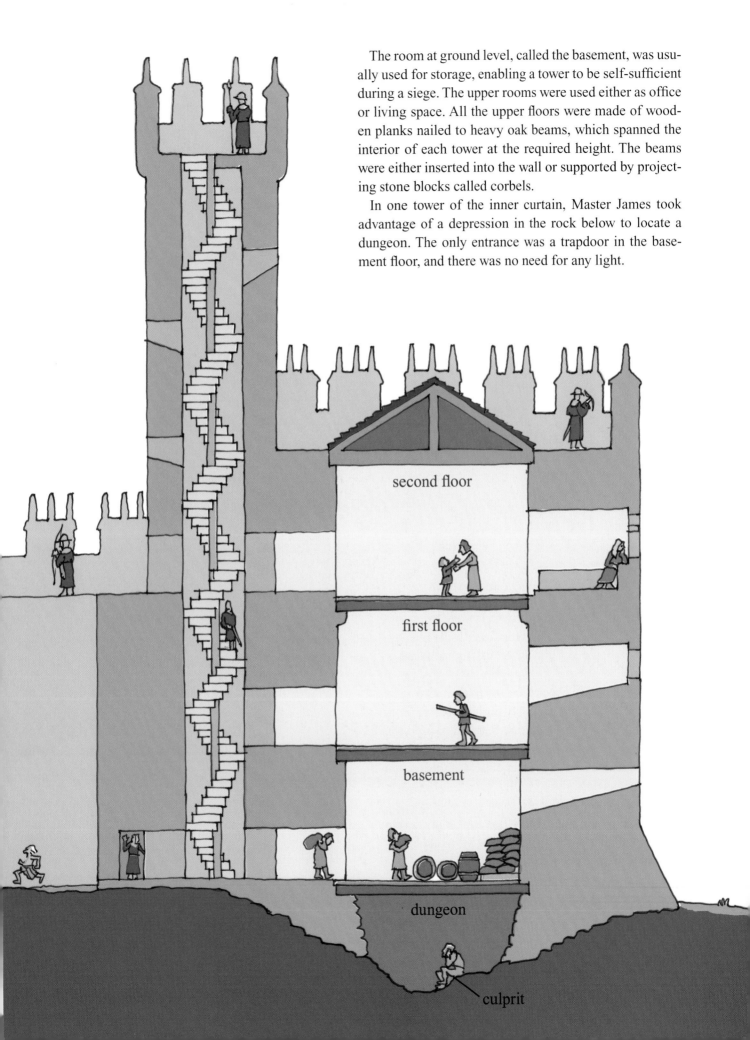

second floor

first floor

basement

dungeon

culprit

The opening at the top of each tower was enclosed by a cone-shaped roof. Its beams or rafters were set into a groove around the inside edge of the tower walk and covered, first with wood and then with either sheets of lead or pieces of slate.

Heat for each of the upper rooms was provided by a large fireplace, built into the wall during construction. Vertical shafts, called flues, carried the smoke from the fireplaces up to chimneys on the tower walks.

At the basement level of the tower closest to the kitchen a second well was dug, and to further insure an adequate supply of water, a tank called a cistern was built into the wall next to the spiral staircase. A lead pipe carried rain water collected in a shallow trough at the base of the roof down to the cistern. A second pipe would deliver the water from the cistern into the kitchen. During hot spells, when the cistern threatened to run dry, it could be filled by hand from the well below.

cistern

wall walk

pipe to
kitchen

During the day, tower rooms were lit almost entirely by the windows. At night oil lamps and candles were required to supplement the light from the fireplace. The walls of the rooms were covered with a thick coat of plaster and either painted, covered with cloth hangings, or both. All the floors, including the dirt floor of the basement, were covered with reeds and sweet-smelling herbs, which were swept out and replaced every month.

Because the windows were the only source of natural light, the recesses behind them were often the size of a small room and contained built-in window seats along each side. For security reasons the windows near the bottom of walls and towers were very narrow, whereas those at the top were quite wide. In the living quarters the windows were fitted with glass and could be closed off by wooden shutters.

In another tower, Master James eliminated the second floor in order to create a high space for the castle's chapel. The apse or altar area was built into a large window recess. An elaborately cut window frame was fitted with panels of specially ordered stained glass. A second recess was cut into the wall at the level of the missing floor. From this space, Lord Kevin and his family would observe the services while the rest of the worshipers stood below.

Many of the tower rooms were just a short distance up or down a spiral staircase from one of the castle's numerous toilets, or garderobes. These had been built into the inner curtain wall and were illuminated and ventilated by a single narrow slit. The seat was simply a slab of stone with a round hole cut in it. The garderobes of the inner curtain were linked to vertical shafts built either within the wall or against it. These shafts led to a cesspit at the foot of the wall, which would be cleaned out periodically. Along the outer curtain, in a minor but potentially effective defensive measure, the seat of each garderobe was supported on stone brackets that projected beyond the exterior face of the wall.

cesspit

By May of 1288 the town wall and its three gatehouses were complete. Not surprisingly, as the security of Aberwyvern increased, so did its population. In addition to farmers who worked the land outside the walls, many of the town's newest inhabitants were merchants and craftsmen and their families. While the first to arrive chose lots close to the public well, all the houses were built right along the unpaved streets to maintain as much grazing and planting land as possible within the walls.

Every house was built of half-timber construction. This meant that the main structure consisted of wooden beams, usually oak, and the spaces between the timbers were filled with wattle and daub. Wattle was a mat of woven sticks and reeds, and daub was the mud or clay smeared on to seal it. Most of the roofs were covered with slate tiles, but a few sheds were still thatched with straw. The ground floor was packed earth, and all the floors were covered with a layer of reeds. Heat was provided by a single fireplace, which also had to light the room, since the window openings were generally very small and usually covered with oiled sheep or goat skin.

Most of Aberwyvern's businessmen, such as Thomas the shoemaker and Oliver the tailor, manufactured and sold their wares from their homes. Their workrooms and shops were located at the front of their houses on the ground floor. During the daytime, horizontal wooden shutters were opened out toward the street. The bottom one dropped down to serve as a counter on which items could be displayed, and the top shutter swung upward and served as an awning. Shops selling such things as produce, fish, and wine were often located near the gates through which those commodities were delivered.

wattle

daub

When the population of Aberwyvern reached several hundred, the town was granted the status of parish and given its own priest. Shortly after his arrival, Father Dominic set out to erect a church on a piece of land donated by Lord Kevin. The gratitude of the townspeople for this recognition was clearly shown by the fact that much of the labor for the building of the church was either freely given or paid for by generous contributions—no small sacrifice for people already working seven days a week. Since it was the only stone building within the town, it soon became both a visual and a social focal point for the community.

With the inner curtain finished, Master James turned his attention to the various permanent buildings that were to occupy the inner ward.

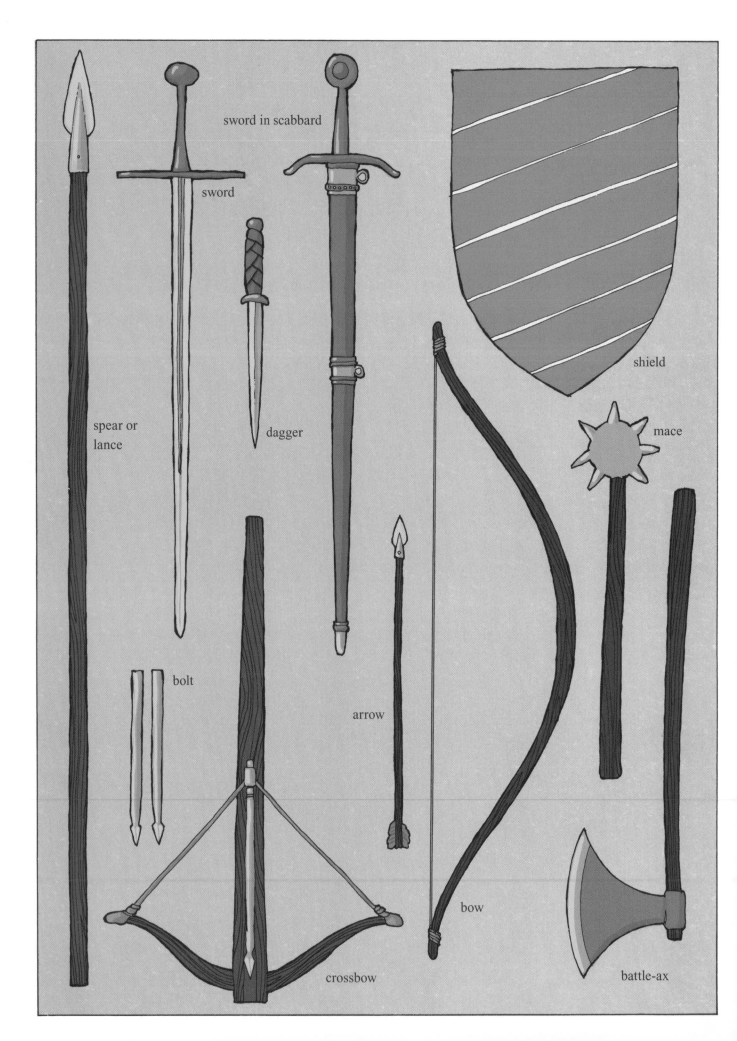

spear or
lance

sword in scabbard

sword

dagger

shield

mace

bolt

arrow

crossbow

bow

battle-ax

The first, intended to house the garrison, was a two-story half-timber structure with a slate roof. The basement was divided between stables and storage rooms, and the second floor served as the living quarters for the men. One of the storage rooms contained many of the garrison's weapons, all of which had been brought from England. Any necessary repairs to the weapons were the responsibility of the blacksmith, whose shop stood nearby.

truss

corbel

The largest new building in the ward, measuring thirty feet wide and more than seventy feet long, was the great hall. It would serve as the general gathering and dining area for the entire population of the castle. Master James located the hall against the inner curtain so that only three new walls would be needed to enclose the space. They were each built of stone and ringed with battlements. The long wall parallel to the inner curtain contained three large windows and a door to the inner ward.

As soon as the walls were finished, carpenters began building the roof. First they spanned the width of the hall with a row of parallel timber frames called trusses, each one arched on the bottom for additional strength and rising to a peak on top. After the trusses were set onto stone corbels embedded in the walls, they were tied together by horizontal beams, covered by wooden planks, and sealed with lead sheets. As soon as the roof was declared watertight, the interior walls were plastered and painted.

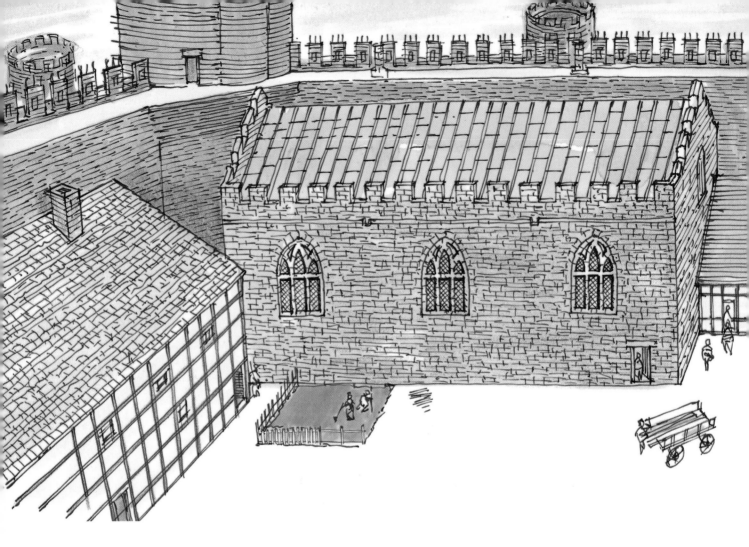

Next to the great hall was the kitchen. It contained a fireplace for cooking and smoking meat, along with a small bake oven, work tables and shelving, hooks for hanging, and a large storage area for various provisions including barrels of wine and ale. Master John, the castle cook, lived in a small apartment above the kitchen with his wife and four children.

Just a few steps from the kitchen door was the main bake house, where the bread for all the castle's residents was produced, and next to it was the granary where sacks of grain were stored before being ground into flour. To prevent dampness and mice from reaching the grain, this structure was supported above the ground on short stone columns.

The remainder of the inner curtain disappeared behind extra guest rooms, additional storerooms, and apartments for William the bailiff, Robert the chaplain, and Lionel, who served as both the barber and the doctor. Squeezed into the corner near the well was a special shed called a mew, in which Lord Kevin's hunting birds were housed.

Although a number of dogs and cats were allowed to roam at will throughout the castle in hopes of controlling the rodent population, one small area of the inner ward was intentionally fenced off. Here Lady Catherine had insisted that a lawn of imported English turf be laid and a garden for flowers and herbs be planted.

In October of 1288, the outer walls of the castle and all its towers were sealed with a coat of lime plaster, giving the entire structure the appearance of having been carved from a single enormous piece of stone, and greatly enhancing its already powerful image.

The following spring saw only a handful of laborers returning to Aberwyvern. There was very little left to do, and the day-to-day maintenance of castle and town wall could now be managed by the craftsmen who had settled permanently in the town.

Shortly after Master James had taken his leave to work on a new project in France, Lady Catherine arrived with her children, attendants, and servants to join Lord Kevin in their new Welsh home.

In 1291, in an attempt to encourage further settlement in this still somewhat hostile land, Lord Kevin granted Aberwyvern a charter. This relieved the residents of the town, present and future, of paying certain taxes, that Kevin could afford to dispense with now that the castle was finished. It also gave the residents the right to elect a mayor and town council, to establish their own court for minor crimes, and to hold a weekly market along the main street.

By 1294, Kevin's castle overlooked a thriving community, and in October of that year King Edward himself, while en route to one of his own castles, paid a visit. On the day of his arrival all the shops and businesses remained closed as the entire population lined the riverbank to catch a glimpse of the royal ships.

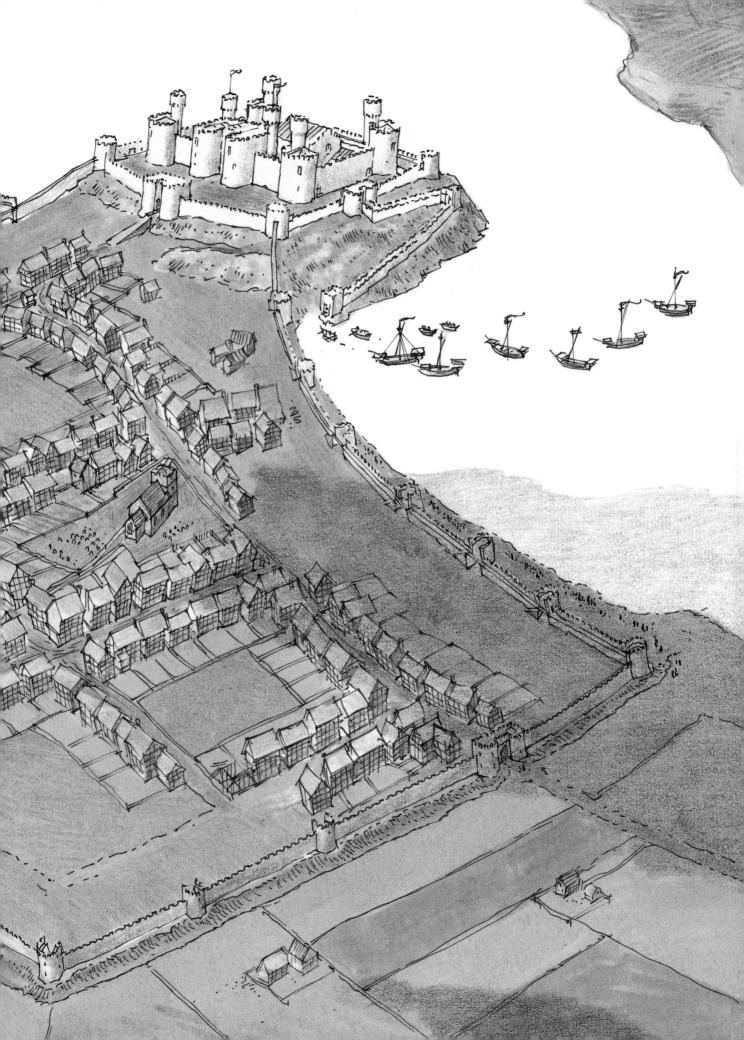

That evening a dinner was held at the castle to which the mayor, the council, and many of the town's prominent merchants were invited. The walls of the great hall were specially hung with colorful banners, and a fresh covering of reeds was spread over the floor. Two large fireplaces that Master James had designed into the curtain wall provided the heat and much of the light. The table for Lord Kevin, Lady Catherine, and their royal guests stood on a raised area at one end of the hall. Everyone else sat at tables set up on the floor close the walls. Food and drink flowed continuously from Master John's kitchen, and entertainment was provided by a variety of musicians, acrobats, and jugglers.

pipe from cistern

Edward was not in Wales for social reasons, however. He had come to quell yet another Welsh rebellion. Before leaving Aberwyvern, he warned Lord Kevin about the situation and encouraged him to prepare for the worst. Since Master James had done all he could to defend against a direct military attack, most of the effort went into preparing for a possible siege. During the next few months, extra large quantities of food and grain were stored away in every available building and room in both castle and town, including the church. A large number of arrows were made, and boulders were collected for dropping off the tops of the walls. To improve the defenders' accuracy, temporary wooden balconies called hoardings were constructed along the battlements.

In July of 1295, both Master James's defenses and the preparations of all the town's residents were put to the test. On the twenty-fourth of that month, the residents of Aberwyvern awoke to find themselves surrounded by a second wall, this one made up of over one thousand Welsh soldiers led by Prince Daffyd of Gwynedd. To prevent the delivery of supplies and the possibility of escape, a string of ships was now anchored just offshore. Through the autumn and winter, the prince bided his time, hoping to starve out his English adversaries. Supplies within the town, however, were holding up well, and the siege seemed to be heading into a second summer. But on June fifth of 1296, after learning that a large English force was gathering along the Welsh border and with his own troops growing increasingly restless, Prince Daffyd ordered a direct attack.

Under cover of darkness, various sections of the town ditch were filled with earth, stones, and logs. Prefabricated sheds were then moved into position up against the wall. They were covered with animal pelts and earth to reduce the chances of their being set on fire. Inside each shed, hanging from chains, was a single heavy tree trunk called a battering ram. The business end of the ram was shaped to a point and capped with iron. As the soldiers rocked the ram back and forth, it began to pound away at the town's fortifications.

Another group of soldiers rolled a pair of tall wooden siege towers up against the hoardings. As archers inside the towers provided some protection, a small drawbridge was lowered onto the hoarding. After two hours of fierce hand-to-hand combat, the attackers withdrew.

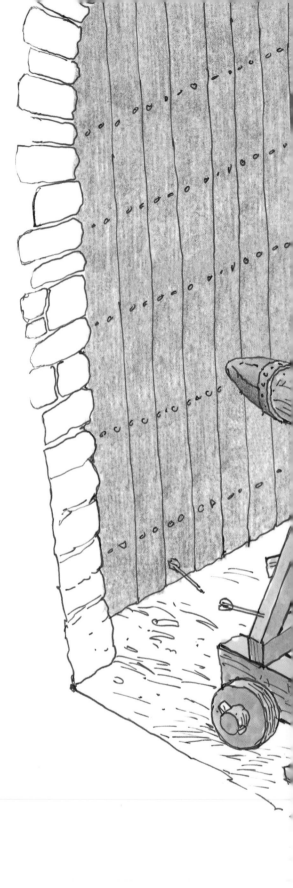

The walls of the town remained under continuous attack for several weeks, making those living behind them increasingly nervous. To add to their problems, Prince Daffyd had ordered a steady aerial barrage from his catapults. Each of these heavy wooden machines was outfitted with a long arm, one end of which was embedded in a highly twisted loop of rope to keep it under great pressure. The other end was shaped like a large spoon. Once the arm had been winched back as far as it would go, the bowl of the spoon was filled with anything from stones and dung to dead animals and scorching embers. When released, the arm would shoot forward at great speed, flinging its unwelcome cargo into the town.

With various objects flying through the air in both directions, the battering rams pounding the walls, and wave after wave of assaults up the charred but still standing siege towers, the battle dragged on. All the while, another group of attackers called sappers was busy digging a tunnel under the wall. As the earth and stone was removed, the top and sides of the tunnel were supported by a framework of logs. The sappers worked around the clock, protected by a wooden structure called a sapper's tent. It too was covered with pelts and earth in an attempt to make it fireproof.

When news reached Prince Daffyd that the English troops were now less than a day's march away, he ordered the supports of the tunnel set on fire. The passage was stuffed with dry wood and straw and fueled with pig carcasses. Flames and smoke poured out of the opening for several hours, as the defenders desperately poured buckets of earth and water from the top of the wall in hopes of dampening the blaze. While a few stones did fall, it eventually became obvious that the wall was not going to collapse. Now facing not only defeat but possible annihilation, Prince Daffyd ordered his men to retreat.

Master James's defenses had done their job well—at least this time—but as King Edward had realized from the start, no amount of military architecture or number of soldiers would ever conquer the people of Wales. They would have to be encouraged to give up the fight on their own. In the months following the uprising, several Welsh families from the surrounding countryside, tired of the bloodshed and interested in sharing Aberwyvern's obvious advantages, were encouraged to settle along the roads outside the gates. On market days and during fairs they were even allowed inside to buy and sell with everyone else. As time passed, the Welsh population grew. Eventually a web of new streets and alleys wrapped itself around the walls, turning Aberwyvern into a town within a town.

Edward's "conquest" of Wales wasn't fully achieved until almost two hundred years after his death when both English and Welsh passed freely through the gates of towns like Aberwyvern, building their houses and observing their individual customs side by side. By then Master James's mighty castle, once an imposing symbol of conquest and warfare, stood roofless and neglected except as an occasional quarry for new buildings, and the walls of the town were now simply a nuisance to its inhabitants rather than a necessity.

CATHEDRAL

CATHEDRAL

INTRODUCTION

For hundreds of years the people of Europe were taught by the church that God was the most important force in their lives. If they prospered, they thanked God for His kindness. If they suffered, they begged for God's mercy, for surely He was punishing them.

In the thirteenth century God was especially good to the people of France. The alliance of a powerful monarchy and an equally powerful clergy helped spread peace, prosperity, and learning across the land. The population grew, crops were plentiful, and business was booming. There were no wars to fight, at least on French soil, and the great plague wasn't even a twinkle in some poor flea's eye. God's blessings were evident, and nowhere more so than in the cities. To express their gratitude and to help insure that He would continue to favor them, many of these vibrant and thriving communities undertook the building of new cathedrals of unprecedented scale and magnificence.

Although the cathedral in this story is imaginary, the methods of its construction correspond closely to the actual construction of a Gothic cathedral. While the builders too are imaginary, their single-mindedness, their spirit, and their incredible courage are typical of the people of twelfth-, thirteenth-, and fourteenth-century Europe whose towering dreams still stand today.

The old cathedral had watched over Chutreaux and its citizens for a hundred years. It was where many of them had been welcomed into the world through baptism, where they had come to learn the teachings of the church, and to be married, and ultimately where they had been brought to be blessed upon their departure from this earth. Its crypt was the final resting place for the city's bishops, as well as for the venerated remains of their very own saint, Etienne de Chutreaux. But as appreciated, even loved, as the building was, it was also beginning to seem a little out of date. The nearby cities of Amiens, Beauvais, and Rouen were already building new cathedrals in which the heavy walls and small windows of earlier days were giving way to slender stone skeletons and vast expanses of glass. Chutreaux was falling behind, and its residents knew it.

The final decision to build a new cathedral was made in the year 1223, after lightning struck and severely damaged the old one. With necessity now added to civic pride, the people of Chutreaux set out to build a structure as inspiring as any in all of France. The new cathedral would be built to the glory of God, and it mattered little that it might take more than one hundred years to construct it.

Although the bishop was the head of the church in Chutreaux, it was a group of clergymen known as the chapter who controlled the money. It was they who hired the widely respected Flemish architect William of Planz to oversee the project and serve as its master builder. William had gained his knowledge of architecture and engineering by visiting and working on many cathedrals not only in France but also in England and Germany.

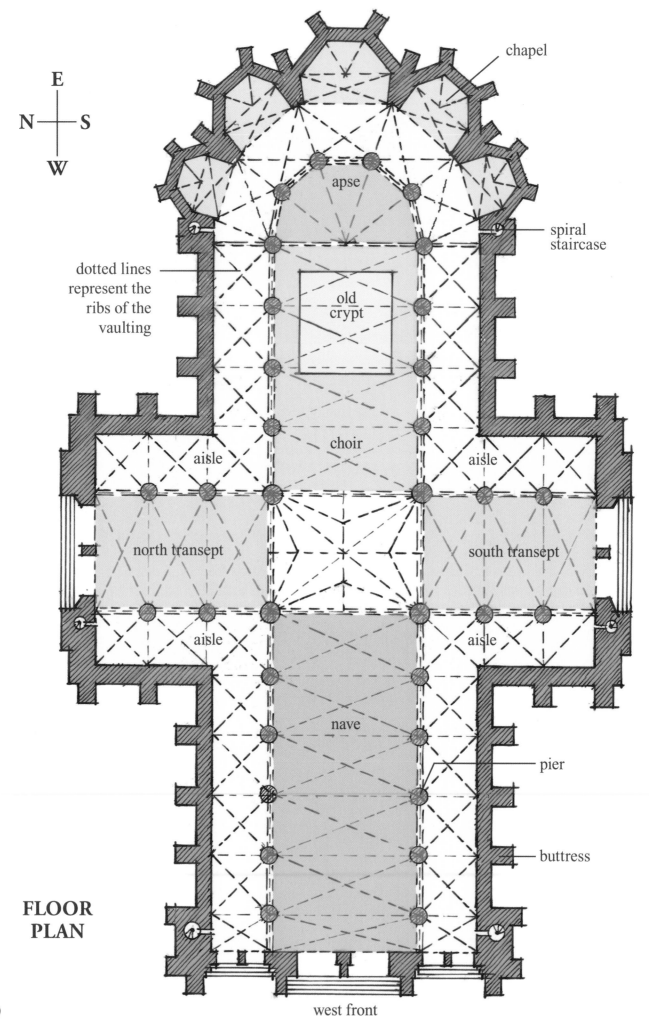

E
N — S
W

chapel

apse

spiral
staircase

dotted lines
represent the
ribs of the
vaulting

old
crypt

choir

aisle   aisle

north transept   south transept

aisle   aisle

nave

pier

buttress

**FLOOR
PLAN**

100

west front

After weeks of planning and sketching, William presented his final designs to the bishop and the chapter. The floor plan, which took the traditional form of a cross, was drawn on a specially prepared sheet of plaster. On a sheet of vellum, he had drawn a cross section of the building to show the main structure from the foundations all the way up to the roof and next to it an elevation of a typical section of the interior wall from floor to ceiling.

On May 24, 1224, the chapter gave its enthusiastic approval to William's design, and work began.

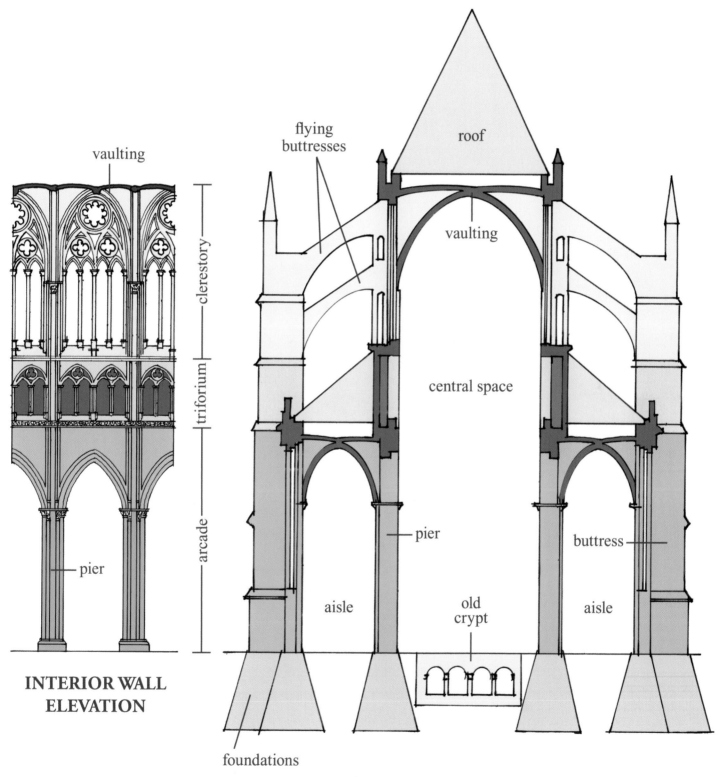

INTERIOR WALL ELEVATION

TYPICAL CROSS SECTION

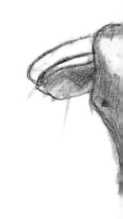

The first task was to gather the necessary workers and the masters who would oversee them. As was customary, William had not come to Chutreaux alone. He was accompanied by several of his most trusted craftsmen, including a master mason, carpenter, and sculptor. The rest of the master craftsmen were hired from the area, including a quarryman, a stonecutter, a mortar maker, a blacksmith, a roofer, and a glassmaker.

In addition to running their particular workshops, each master was responsible for the training of apprentices, or assistants who one day hoped to become masters themselves. Most of the heavy work was done by laborers, men with no particular skill. Some came from Chutreaux, some from the surrounding countryside.

lever

saw

mallet
and chisel

dividers

measuring
stick

pickax

mistake

square

ax

two-man
saw

saws

adze

Most of the tools used by the various craftsmen were
made of wood and iron. All the metalwork was done by
a blacksmith, and the wooden pieces were produced by
skilled woodworkers.

wood chisel

brace

auger

bit

By mid-June, laborers were busy clearing the site for the new cathedral. Beginning at the eastern end where the apse and choir would eventually stand, they removed all that remained of the old building except for the crypt, which, with its precious contents, would be incorporated into the new structure. As the new cathedral was to be much larger than its predecessor, a number of houses, including the bishop's palace, which had been damaged during the fire, had to be either demolished or dismantled and relocated.

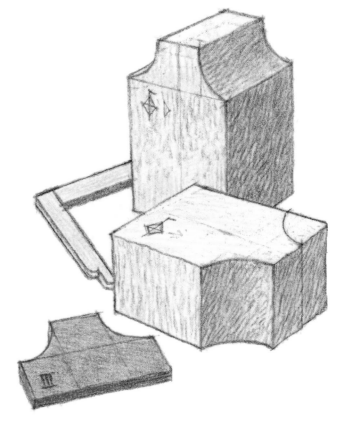

Even while William was still designing, his master quarryman had been touring a number of sites in the Somme valley, an area rich in limestone. After comparing the quality of the stone, he made arrangements on behalf of the chapter to rent an existing quarry for the duration of the project. As soon as the plans were approved, he ordered the construction of several new stonecutting sheds and a forge where the blacksmith could make and repair tools.

As blocks of stone were pried free of the quarry face, laborers delivered them to one of the workshops, where stonecutters chiseled out the rough shape following a pattern or template supplied by the master mason. Each stone was marked twice, once to show which stonecutter had actually shaped it so that he would be paid, and once to show its final location in the cathedral.

At the same time, a master carpenter and several of his apprentices, along with one hundred and fifty laborers, were busily harvesting timber in the forest of Chantilly for the construction of scaffolding, workshops, and hoisting machines.

William wanted to be sure that by the time construction began, a steady supply of building material would always be available. Most of the stone and timber arrived by boat at the city dock, where it was loaded onto waiting carts and hauled up to the site by teams of oxen. The first sacks of lime from a local kiln were also beginning to pile up under the sloping roof of the mortar makers' shed.

As soon as the east end of the site had been sufficiently cleared, William had marked out the location of the apse and choir with wooden stakes. Now teams of laborers were busily digging the holes for the foundations, which would support the building and prevent it from settling unevenly. Around the edge of the site, and a safe distance from the excavations, and the small mountains of earth they produced, carpenters built a number of workshops and sheds in which the craftsmen could eat, rest, and work in bad weather. They also built a second forge for the production of tools and nails.

The blessing of the first foundation stone on April 14, 1225, began a construction project almost as massive as that of the cathedral itself, but one that would disappear entirely below the ground.

The first layer of foundation stones was set on a bed of pebbles and clay at the bottom of the excavation. As the blocks were nudged into place, masons troweled a thin layer of mortar between them. This precise mixture of sand, lime, and water was produced by mortar men and delivered to the masons by laborers.

With his level, the master mason continually checked to make sure each course of stone was perfectly horizontal. Any carelessness in the construction of the foundations could endanger the structure that would eventually stand on top of them.

As the masons gradually worked their way around the choir, carpenters built a roof over the crypt to protect it from the rain and snow.

When the first section of foundation was completed and its mortar had sufficiently hardened, work began on the walls above. The walls of a Gothic cathedral like Chutreaux's either rest directly on the foundations or on an arcade, a row of arches supported by massive columns called piers, which have their own foundations.

For sections of solid wall, the stone mason would actually construct two parallel walls and then fill the space between them with concrete, a mixture of mortar and small stones. It would have been too expensive to build walls of solid stone. The main piers, on the other hand, were built entirely of stone with no infill, all the way up to the triforium.

The vertical mullions and intricate tracery that made up the framework of the windows, all of which was carefully cut from templates, were cemented into place as the walls were being built. But even before the window level was reached, wooden scaffolding had become a necessity for supporting hoists as well as movable platforms for the workers. The scaffolding was made of poles lashed together with rope, and the platforms, called hurdles, were made of woven twigs.

Next to one of the chapels surrounding the apse, masons were building a spiral staircase to carry workers, tools, and even some materials up to the triforium. By the time the cathedral was finished, several such staircases would be in place, some of which reached all the way to the roof.

By 1235 many of the piers of the arcade were complete and work began on the arches that would link them. These were built of wedge-shaped blocks of stone called voussoirs over temporary wooden frames called centerings. Once the wall above each arch was in place and its mortar had set, the centering could be lowered and used elsewhere.

buttress

pier extension

aisle

pier

The smaller arches of the triforium as well as the narrow passageway behind them were built next on top of the arcade. As each section of the triforium was finished, it was tied to the top of the outer wall by a wooden roof. The aisle between the arcade and the outer wall was then covered by a vaulted ceiling. Once again wooden centerings were used—this time to build the arches that would help support the vaulting.

By the summer of 1242, the pier extensions and window tracery of the clerestory were visible. Given the scarcity and expense of very tall timbers, the scaffolding required for everything above the triforium was supported by the walls themselves rather than the floor.

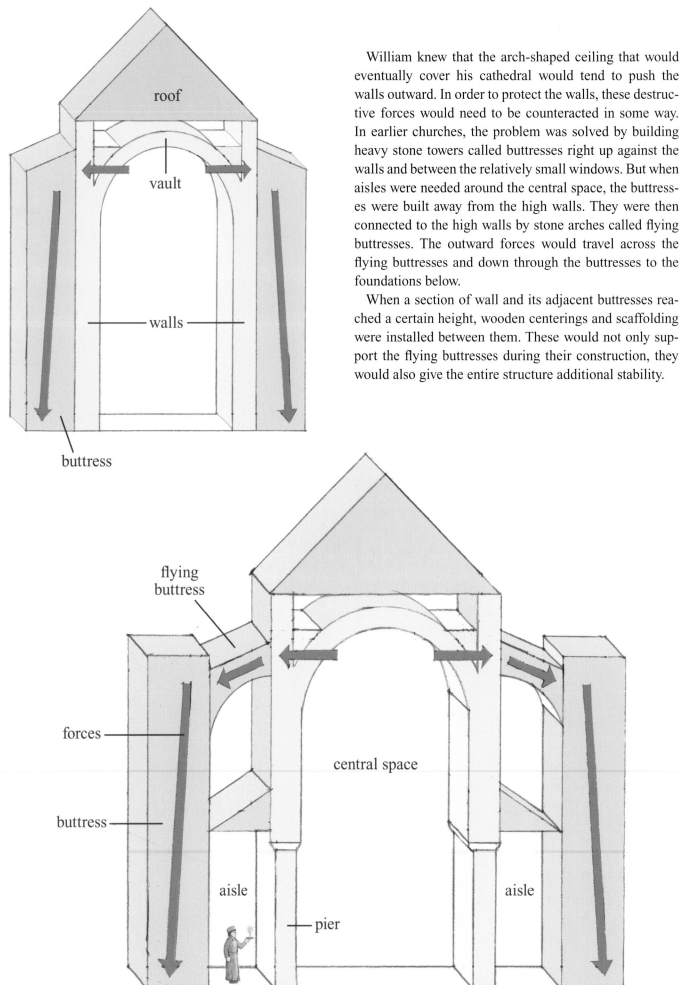

William knew that the arch-shaped ceiling that would eventually cover his cathedral would tend to push the walls outward. In order to protect the walls, these destructive forces would need to be counteracted in some way. In earlier churches, the problem was solved by building heavy stone towers called buttresses right up against the walls and between the relatively small windows. But when aisles were needed around the central space, the buttresses were built away from the high walls. They were then connected to the high walls by stone arches called flying buttresses. The outward forces would travel across the flying buttresses and down through the buttresses to the foundations below.

When a section of wall and its adjacent buttresses reached a certain height, wooden centerings and scaffolding were installed between them. These would not only support the flying buttresses during their construction, they would also give the entire structure additional stability.

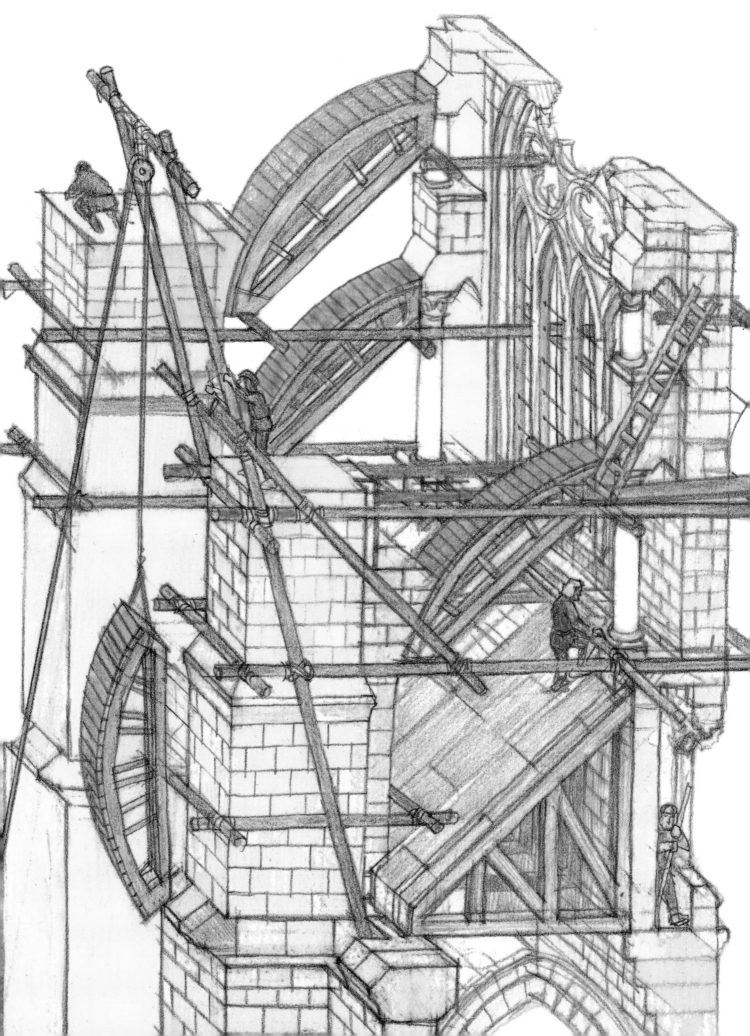

Even as tracery was being installed, window makers were already at work preparing for the time when they would replace the masons on the scaffolding. Most of the windows would use a combination of clear glass—to illuminate the interior space—along with small areas of decorative stained glass. A number of special windows to be filled entirely with stained glass had also been ordered. Because of their expense, these windows were paid for by wealthy individuals or professional organizations.

blow pipe

punti

130

Since these windows were meant to tell specific stories, the window makers and clergymen worked closely together on their design.

The glass used in all the windows was made from a combination of beechwood ash and washed sand melted together at high temperatures. To achieve the different colors, particular kinds of metals, vegetation, and even old glass were added to the mix. All the glass was produced in workshops located near surrounding forests, where plenty of wood was available for fueling the furnaces.

There were two main ways of making the glass, but both began by first scooping up a ball of molten glass on the end of a hollow pipe and blowing air into it. In one method the glass was blown up like a balloon before being transferred to a solid pipe called a punti. The blow pipe was then cut free and the sphere, now with a hole in it, was spun quickly, which forced it to open up into a flat circular shape. It was then removed from the punti and allowed to cool. The second method involved blowing up the glass while simultaneously rolling it on a hard surface to form a cylinder. When the cylinder reached the right size, the ends were cut off and it was sliced down the middle and opened to form a flat sheet.

131

At each window maker's shop, a full-size plan for a section of a window was first drawn on a whitewashed bench. Every piece of glass was laid over this pattern before being cut to the exact size and shape using a pointed steel rod called a grozing iron. Individual pieces of glass were usually quite small, but when several pieces were joined together using specially cast strips of lead, they could form sections as large as thirty inches square. As each window section was finished, copper rods were attached to the outer face to provide additional rigidity against the wind.

On the scaffolding, window makers installed iron bars between the mullions and tracery to support the weight of the glass panels and to hold them in place. Although single pieces of glass were usually no larger than eight inches square, the finished windows could easily reach heights of forty feet or more.

In November, as in every previous winter, the stone-work was covered with straw and dung to prevent frost from cracking the mortar before it had completely dried. While many of the masons went home during the coldest months, those apprentices who couldn't afford the time off worked in the quarries. Stonecutters and sculptors took up residence either in workshops or in smaller sheds between the buttresses of the choir, which were a little easier to heat. They continued shaping stones and tracery or carving capitals and statues in preparation for the return of the masons in the spring.

134

By 1247 the 140-foot-high walls that surrounded the choir were finished and in the autumn of that year work began on the roof, which would eventually add another fifty feet to the overall height of the building.

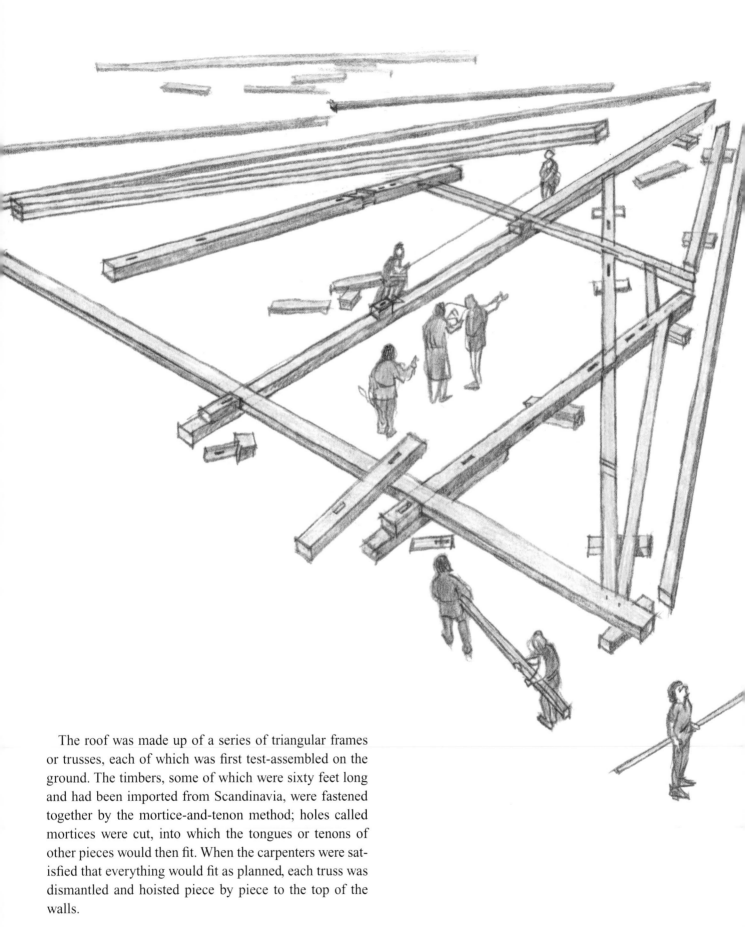

The roof was made up of a series of triangular frames or trusses, each of which was first test-assembled on the ground. The timbers, some of which were sixty feet long and had been imported from Scandinavia, were fastened together by the mortice-and-tenon method; holes called mortices were cut, into which the tongues or tenons of other pieces would then fit. When the carpenters were satisfied that everything would fit as planned, each truss was dismantled and hoisted piece by piece to the top of the walls.

Once the crossbeams were in place, a windlass was set on top of them to hoist the rest of the timber and help in setting up the trusses. As the various pieces were maneuvered into their final position, each mortice and tenon was locked together with oak pegs. When the completed trusses were fastened together, additional timbers were installed, to which rows of wooden slats were then nailed. Before being covered with sheets of lead, all of the timber was coated with pitch to prevent rotting.

By the spring of 1253 the roof was finished and the choir was ready to receive its vaulting. This stone ceiling would spring from the walls about a hundred feet off the ground and rise to a height of thirty feet. Robert of Cormont, who had replaced the aging William as master builder, supervised the erection of new scaffolding high up above the choir on which masons, mortar makers, and carpenters could safely work.

It was during the construction of the scaffolding that the bishop of Chutreaux died. Work stopped for seven days, and on the fourteenth of July 1253, his body was interred in a new tomb in the old crypt. On the fifteenth of September work was interrupted once again, this time for the installation of Roland of Clermont as the new bishop of Chutreaux.

Two types of machines would be used to lift the stones and concrete to the roof for the construction of the vaults. The first was the windlass, of which there were several already in place, and the second was the great wheel. It was large enough so that one or two men could stand inside. Through its center ran a long axle to which the hoisting rope was fastened. As the men walked forward both the wheel and the axle turned, winding up the rope. The great wheel was capable of lifting very heavy loads, the first of which were the large centerings that would temporarily support the vaulting until it could stand on its own.

keystone

voussoir

rib

One by one the precisely cut voussoirs were placed on the centering and mortared together by the masons. When a number of ribs met at the crown—the highest point of the arch—they were locked in place by the insertion of a keystone. A year later, with the mortar sufficiently hardened, the ceiling itself, called the webbing, could be built. Two teams, each with a mason and a carpenter, worked simultaneously from both sides of a vault. The carpenter first installed narrow wooden frames called lagging on top of the centering and across the space between the ribs. The masons then laid webbing stones on top of the lagging. They used the lightest stone possible to reduce the weight.

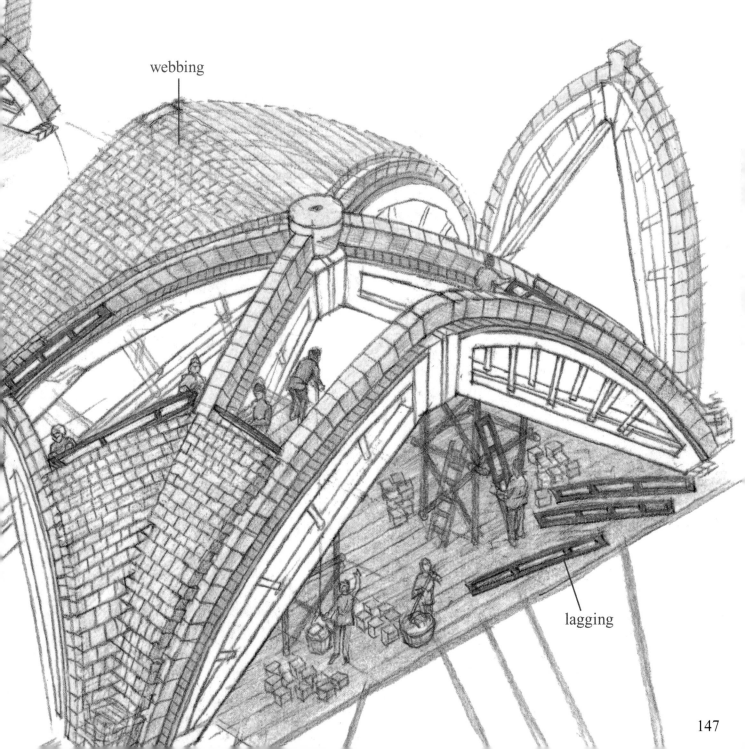

webbing

lagging

Finally a four-inch layer of concrete was poured over the entire vault to prevent any cracking between the stones. The deep cone-shaped spaces left between the ends of each arch and the wall were filled with pieces of webbing and rubble to further strengthen the vault against the outward thrust of the arches.

When the centering and lagging was eventually lowered and moved to the next bay to repeat the entire process, the underside of the webbing was coated with plaster on which lines were carefully painted to give the impression that all the stones were more or less regular. Since no one on the ground would notice the difference, this was primarily done for God's eyes.

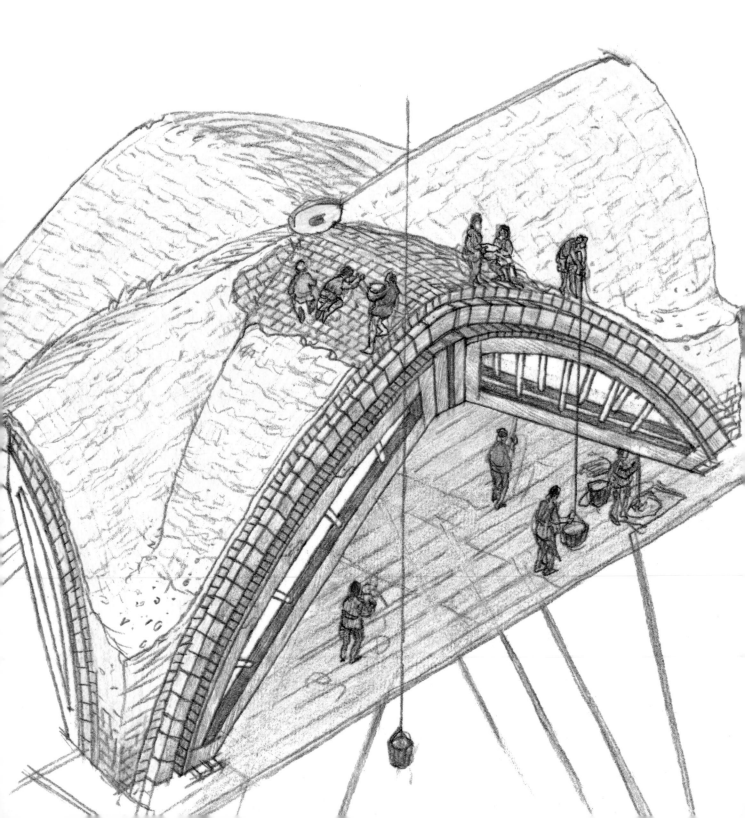

By the time the vaulting was complete, so were all the flying buttresses. The buttresses themselves were capped with steep pinnacles to add extra weight, and various carved stone creatures were set in place to ward off evil spirits. Some of these grotesque creatures also served as downspouts called gargoyles. When it rained, water from the roof would travel across the upper flying buttresses and out through the mouths of the gargoyles onto the ground below.

Once the scaffolding had been removed, the covering over the crypt was dismantled. At the same time, a high temporary wall was built to seal off the choir from the rest of the construction so that it could be safely and immediately used for services.

In June of 1264 during the annual Pentecost celebrations the choir was dedicated with great festivity. But within two years the chapter had run out of money and almost all work on the building was halted. After doubling his own financial commitment to the project, Bishop Roland encouraged the cannons and citizens of Chutreaux to follow his example. And to stir the generosity of those well beyond the city walls, he also decided that various relics from the crypt should be displayed throughout the surrounding countryside for a period of five years.

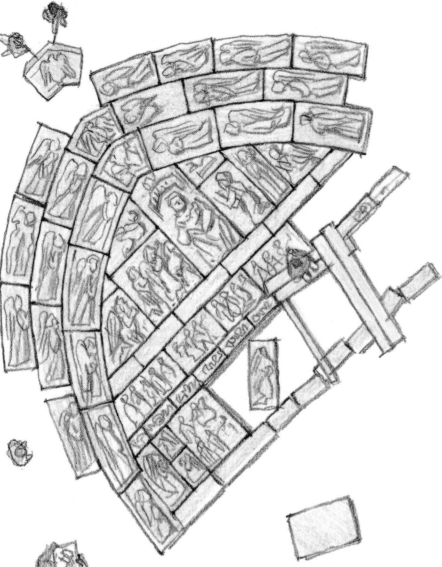

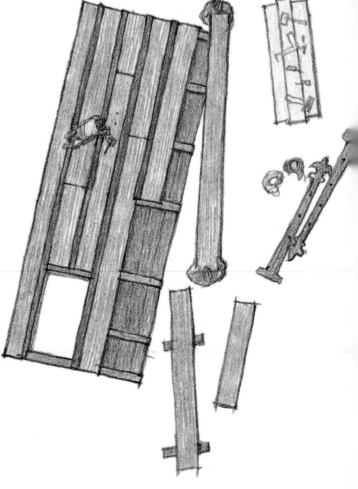

With money finally flowing back into the coffers, work resumed on the next part of the cathedral, the transept. Its north and south ends were enclosed by massive walls, each housing a spiral staircase that went up one hundred and forty feet to the roof. Set into both walls high above an imposing entryway was a large rose window.

Voussoirs were carved to form the arched gables over the doors and a tympanum—a semicircular sculpted panel—was carved to go above the doors. Once in place, the various carvings were painted with vibrant colors. The doors themselves were made of heavy planks joined with cross ribs. One of the blacksmiths had made all the nails for the door and a master metalworker had created the bolts, locks, and hinges.

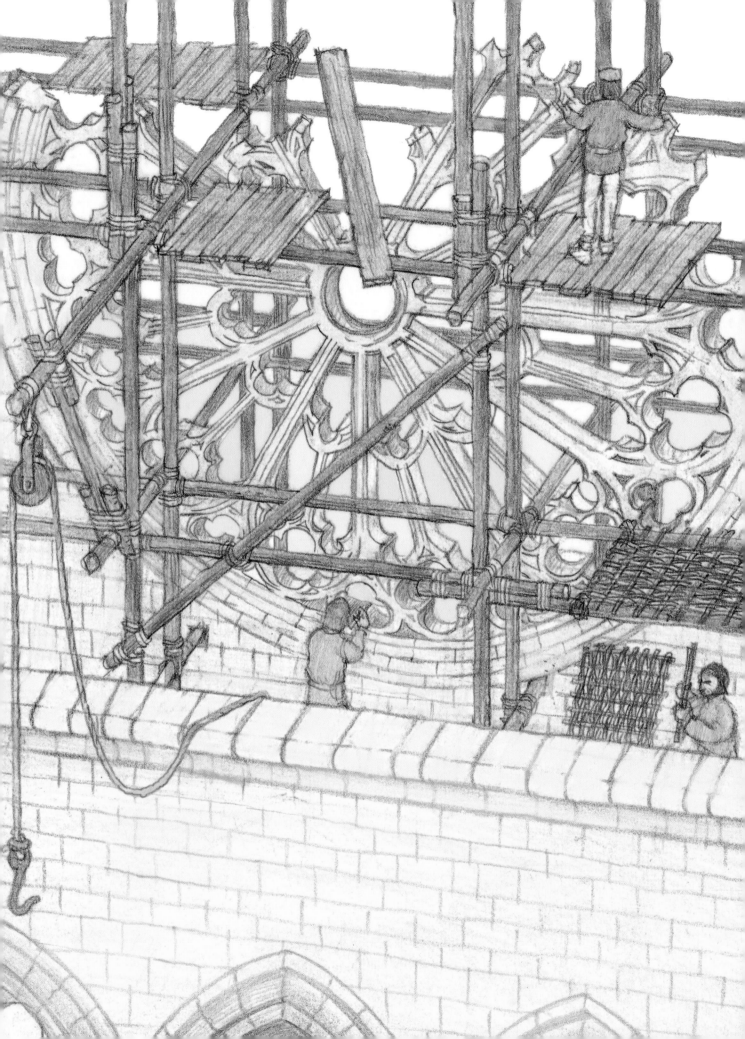

Sixteen years would elapse between the dedication of the choir and that of the transept. After a week of festivities, Master Robert and his workers turned their attention to the piers and buttresses of the nave. At the same time, a group of highly skilled carpenters and roofers a hundred and ninety feet above them began assembling the 150 foot-tall spire. This wood-framed structure was covered with sheets of lead and decorated with sculpture and ornaments.

In 1282, as the spire neared completion, Bishop Roland, who had been so eager to preside over its dedication, succumbed to injuries sustained while touring the site.

Out of gratitude for his leadership and great personal generosity, it was decided that he should be buried in the cathedral itself rather than in the crypt. His tomb was built in the aisle adjacent to the choir.

Over the next twenty years construction gradually proceeded westward. By 1302 the centering was in place for the last section of vaulting and within a year the nave itself was finished. As work began on the west front with its two towers and three entrances, the people of Chutreaux dared at last to imagine the completion of their splendid cathedral. But there would be one more small test of their patience and determination.

News arrived from the quarry that the stone now being extracted was no longer of sufficient quality. The remaining building material would have to come from another quarry several miles farther away. As funds were already stretched, the added expense was greeted with understandable dismay. Since fewer craftsmen could now be afforded, the pace of work slowed considerably.

But it never stopped, and for another twelve years the
façade climbed slowly but steadily skyward.

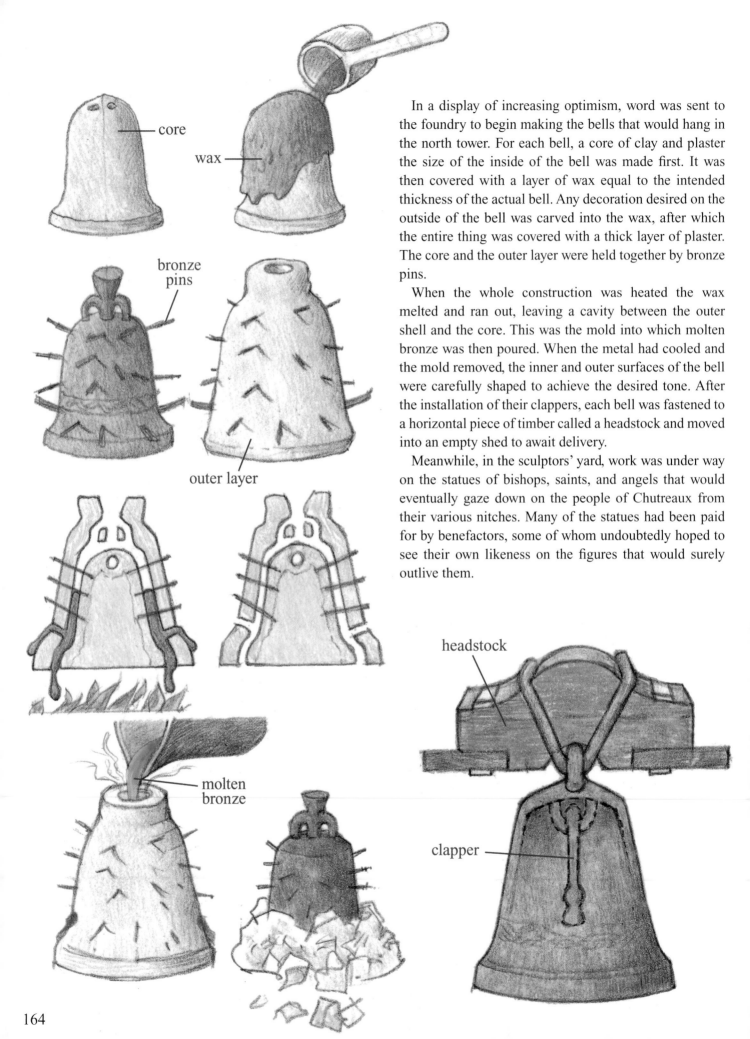

core

wax

bronze
pins

outer layer

molten
bronze

headstock

clapper

In a display of increasing optimism, word was sent to the foundry to begin making the bells that would hang in the north tower. For each bell, a core of clay and plaster the size of the inside of the bell was made first. It was then covered with a layer of wax equal to the intended thickness of the actual bell. Any decoration desired on the outside of the bell was carved into the wax, after which the entire thing was covered with a thick layer of plaster. The core and the outer layer were held together by bronze pins.

When the whole construction was heated the wax melted and ran out, leaving a cavity between the outer shell and the core. This was the mold into which molten bronze was then poured. When the metal had cooled and the mold removed, the inner and outer surfaces of the bell were carefully shaped to achieve the desired tone. After the installation of their clappers, each bell was fastened to a horizontal piece of timber called a headstock and moved into an empty shed to await delivery.

Meanwhile, in the sculptors' yard, work was under way on the statues of bishops, saints, and angels that would eventually gaze down on the people of Chutreaux from their various nitches. Many of the statues had been paid for by benefactors, some of whom undoubtedly hoped to see their own likeness on the figures that would surely outlive them.

164

The bells were eventually hung from a sturdy timber framework called a bell frame. Both were protected from the elements by a wooden roof and shutters. A wheel attached to each headstock was connected to a long piece of rope. When a bell ringer below pulled on the rope, the bell rocked back and forth, forcing the clapper to strike the wall. The ringing could be heard for miles.

By midsummer 1314, the cathedral was complete, and on August 19 the bishop and the chapter led a great procession through the narrow streets, returning with the entire population of the city.

Inside the cathedral, colored light streamed through the windows while candles flickered beneath the arches of the triforium. As the choir began to sing, the building filled with beautiful sounds and everyone there, most of them grandchildren and great-grandchildren of the men who had laid the foundations, was filled with tremendous awe and great joy.

For ninety years the people of Chutreaux had shared a single dream, and at last it had been realized.

MOSQUE

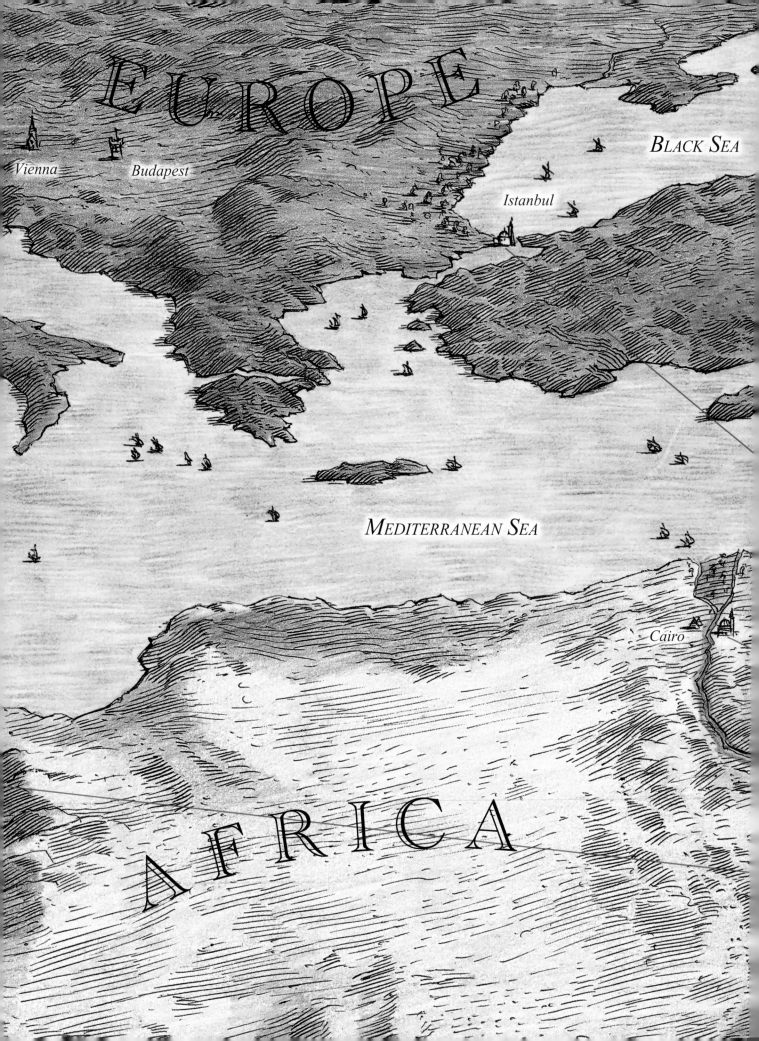

EUROPE

Vienna   Budapest

BLACK SEA

Istanbul

MEDITERRANEAN SEA

AFRICA

Cairo

MOSQUE

Damascus

Jerusalem

Baghdad

A S I A

RED SEA

Mecca

INTRODUCTION

By the middle of the sixteenth century, the Ottomans had built the largest Muslim empire in the world. With superior forces on land and sea, a series of sultans had extended its borders from Algiers in the west to Baghdad in the east, from the outskirts of Vienna in the north to beyond Mecca in the south. With the establishment of military dominance came the inevitable building of trade and cultural links, and with these spread the message of Islam and its five pillars—faith, prayer, charity, fasting, and pilgrimage.

One indication of the empire's unrivaled power was the phenomenal wealth that found its way into the sultans' treasury as well as into the pockets of Istanbul's most influential citizens. For these individuals, however, adherence to the principle of charity was further encouraged by laws that prevented the bequeathing of one's entire fortune to one's children. It became a well-established practice, therefore, for the richest members of society to endow charitable foundations to channel their personal wealth into a variety of religious, educational, social, and civic activities. These foundations would require a number of specific buildings all grouped into an architectural complex called a kulliye.

The centerpiece of each kulliye was the mosque, and by the fifteenth century, the basic form of the Ottoman mosque was well established. It consisted of an open prayer hall—ideally a perfect cube covered by an equally perfect hemisphere-shaped dome, a covered porch or portico, an arcaded courtyard similar in area to the prayer hall itself, a fountain, and a slender minaret (usually more than one if the mosque was built by royalty). Over time the domed cube became the standard form for all the buildings of a kulliye, regardless of their function.

The design and construction of most of the great Ottoman architecture of the sixteenth century was overseen by one man, an architect and engineer named Sinan. For almost fifty years, he and his assistants created buildings, bridges, and aqueducts all across the empire. By the time of his death at the age of one hundred, he had personally served as architect for some three hundred structures in Istanbul alone.

Although the building complex in this story is fictional, as are its patron and architect, the individual structures are modeled directly on Sinan's work in and around Istanbul, Turkey, between 1540 and 1580.

Admiral Suha Mehmet Pasa had done well by war. For more than thirty years his successful naval campaigns had made him a highly respected member of the Ottoman aristocracy, a favorite of two sultans, and a very rich man. For most of his life his eyes were firmly fixed on the borders of the empire he worked so valiantly to protect. But as another decade slipped away, he found himself confronting less familiar boundaries—those of his own mortality. As a devout Muslim, the admiral understood that all the blessings and riches that had been showered upon him were not due to his own efforts as much as to the will of God. The time had come to display both his faith and his gratitude in a way befitting a man of his standing.

So it was that one October day in the year 1595, a senior member of Sultan Mehmet III's Corps of Court Architects named Akif Agha was summoned to the admiral's home to discuss the various buildings that would house the activities of the admiral's proposed foundation. In addition to a mosque with its adjacent tomb, the complex would include a medrese, a school for religious education; an imaret, a soup kitchen for the preparation and distribution of food; a hamam, a public bathhouse; and a cesme, a public fountain to provide fresh drinking water.

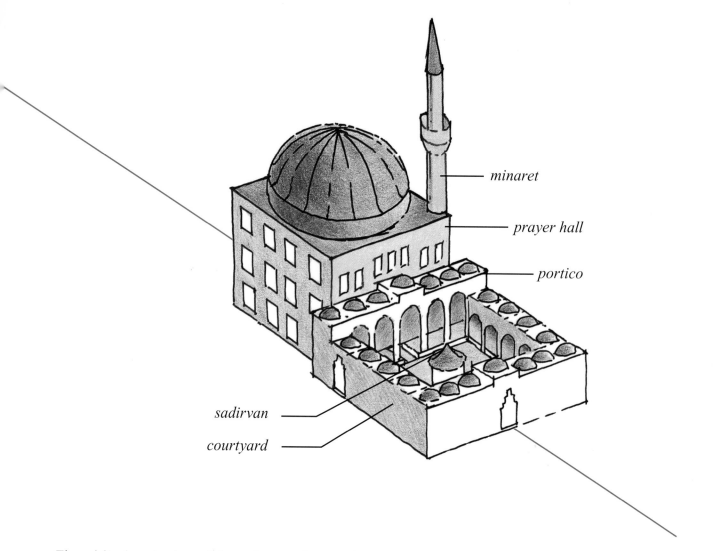

minaret

prayer hall

portico

sadirvan

courtyard

The spiritual centerpiece of the entire complex was the mosque, and the heart of the mosque was its prayer hall. It was with the design of this space in which the faithful would gather that Akif Agha began. There were a number of absolute requirements, the most important of which was that the front wall, or kibla wall, of this room must face Mecca. When praying, the congregation would assemble in rows parallel to and facing the kibla wall and also the holy city and its most important shrine, the Kaaba. At floor level in the center of the kibla wall was the mihrab—a niche symbolizing the entrance to paradise. It was from in front of the mihrab that the imam would lead the congregation in prayer. The kibla itself is an imaginary line that points toward and radiates from Mecca. The kibla wall was placed perpendicular to the kibla, and the mihrab stood right on top of it.

Directly opposite the mihrab was the portal—the main entrance to the prayer hall. Protecting the portal outside and providing covered space for latecomers to Friday services was a high portico, and beyond it an arcaded courtyard. In the center of the courtyard stood the sadirvan—the fountain at which the faithful would wash their hands and feet

before entering the prayer hall. Like the mihrab, the main portal and the sadirvan were also located on the kibla.

Akif Agha reminded his young apprentices that when working with a large dome it was necessary to think from the ground up and from the top down at the same time. There were two basic problems, the first of which was simple geometry. How does one support a circular roof over a square room without filling that room with walls or columns? The solution was a system of piers and arches. The piers were placed around the perimeter of the square and tied together by a ring of arches.

The second problem was one of structure. Because of the dome's hemispherical shape, there are forces within it trying to push the sides outward. While the piers and arches could support the great weight of a masonry dome, they could not, on their own, counteract these horizontal forces. To solve this problem the sides of the dome were strengthened. Then, to channel the remaining forces safely down through the piers and walls to the foundations below, extra weight was added to the tops of the piers and the ring of arches was buttressed by a series of semidomes.

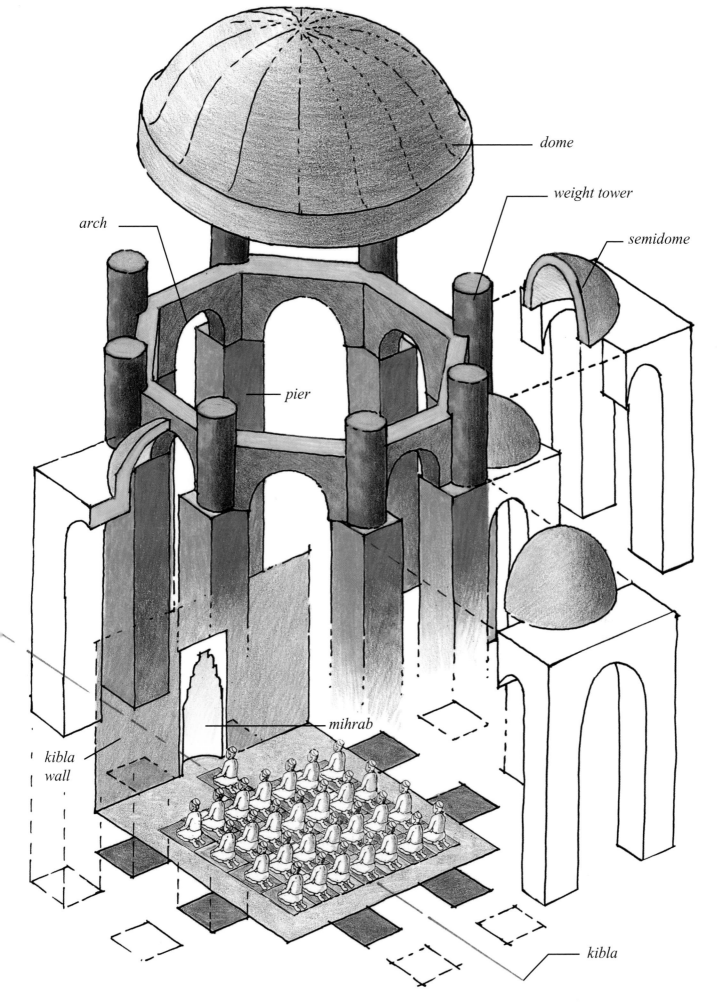

dome

weight tower

semidome

arch

pier

mihrab

kibla
wall

kibla

181

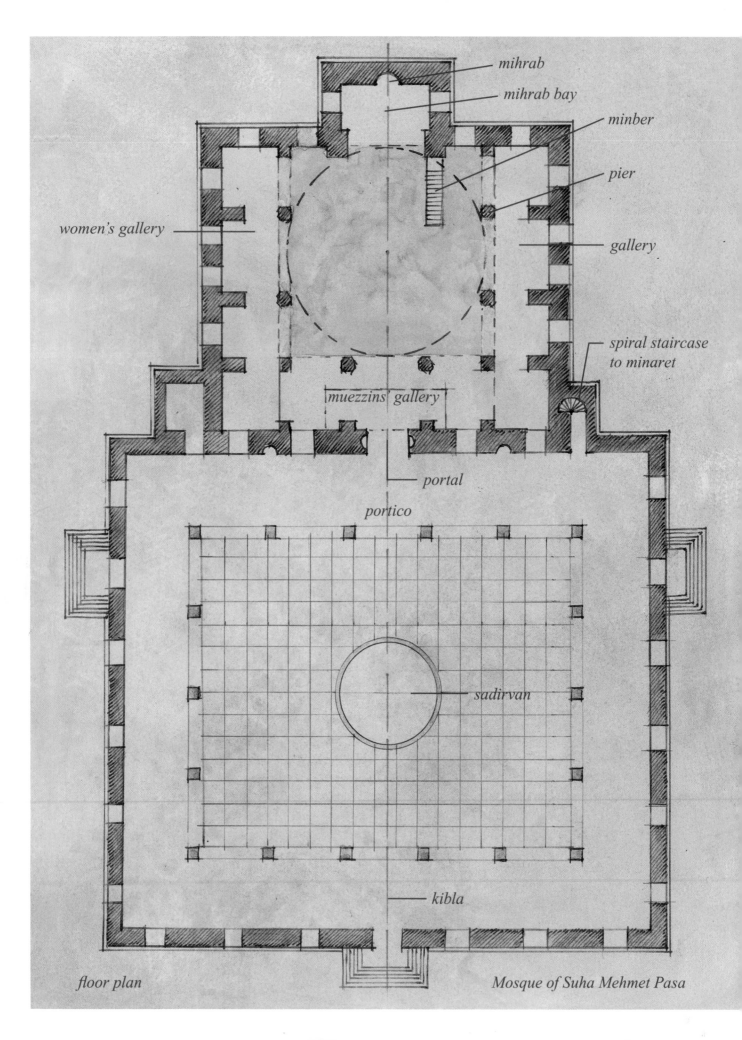

mihrab

mihrab bay

minber

pier

gallery

spiral staircase
to minaret

women's gallery

muezzins' gallery

portal

portico

sadirvan

kibla

floor plan

Mosque of Suha Mehmet Pasa

The design Agha finally presented to the admiral in January of 1596 called for a prayer hall seventy feet wide and fifty-six feet deep. To draw more attention to the mihrab, the architect set it into its own bay, which he pushed out from the central space. Then, to give as many worshipers as possible access to the kibla wall, he extended it on both sides of the central square. He provided raised galleries along the side walls—one of them for women—and one at the rear of the prayer hall for the muezzins who would chant the words of the Koran. This mosque was to be large enough to accommodate Friday services, certainly the most important religious gathering of the week and probably the most important secular one too. The sermons at these services would be delivered from the second to last step of a high pulpit called a minber. The traditional placement of the minber was to one side of the mihrab, or in this case the mihrab bay.

The dome would be forty-two feet in diameter and its crest would stand sixty-three feet above the floor. The open courtyard space within the colonnade was roughly equal to the area of the prayer hall, and the minaret would rise to a height of one hundred ten feet. With their patron's enthusiastic approval and encouragement, Agha and his staff immediately began the detailed planning.

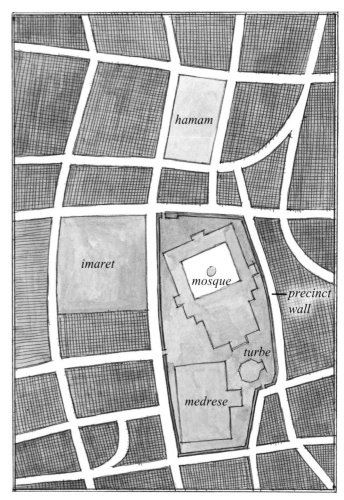

Kulliye of Suha Mehmet Pasa

By early spring, negotiations had been concluded for a site that fulfilled all of the admiral's wishes. In addition to being obtained for a good price, it was blessed with an excellent view of the harbor and benefited from the steady breezes on which his ships had so often set sail. Not everyone shared His Excellency's nostalgia for breezes, however. All too often, these very same winds would fan small fires into raging infernos such as the one that less than ten years earlier had reduced this entire neighborhood to rubble and left its population in despair.

To oversee the day-in, day-out activities at the site, Agha hired a man named Huseyin Bey to serve as the superintendent of building. Bey soon had gangs of unskilled laborers clearing the site and digging foundation trenches for the wall that would enclose both the mosque and the medrese in a single precinct. He also set aside a space near one of the entrances to this precinct for toilets and assigned temporary areas to each of the building trades for their work sheds and supplies.

Since relatively few large building projects were under way at the time, Agha had little trouble finding the necessary workers. At least half of them would be skilled craftsmen and artists, and half of this group, particularly the bricklayers and blacksmiths, would most likely be Christians. Most of the stonemasons, carpenters, roofers, and window makers would be Muslims. Hundreds of additional skilled and unskilled laborers, boatmen, wagon drivers, night watchmen, storekeepers, and porters, would also be hired. More than a thousand workers would be employed on and around the site at any given time, and to take advantage of the long summer days, that number would most certainly increase.

Early on the morning of June 5, 1596, surveyors, working from various charts, established the placement of the kibla and marked it on the site with wooden stakes. Next they located the kibla wall and eventually laid out the rest of the prayer hall.

Less than a week later, excavation of the deep trenches for the foundations of the prayer hall was begun. Although the admiral would occasionally express frustration with the amount of money being spent on foundations that no one would ever see, Agha assured him that in a city such as Istanbul, with its long history of earthquakes, the quality of these buried walls was every bit as important as that of the walls they would support aboveground. If the admiral couldn't refute the logic behind Agha's preparations, he could at least speed them up. He assigned several hundred galley slaves from a nearby garrison to help with the digging. Once a reliable surface had been reached, a thick level base of rubble and cement was then created, upon which the foundation walls would be built.

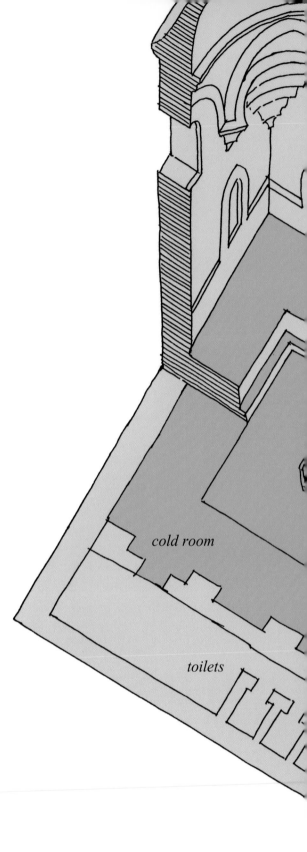

Two blocks away from the main site, near an existing well, another group of workers was digging the foundations for the hamam. The admiral had decided that the baths should be completed as soon as possible for the use of his workers. The bathhouse Agha designed followed the sequence first established in ancient times in which bathers moved from cold room to warm room to hot room. In the cold room, they would undress and relax, perhaps sipping coffee or mineral water before bathing. A fountain in the center of the room would fill the air with its soothing sound. The actual cleansing process began in the warm room and continued in the hot room, where bathers could either wash at one of the basins or simply sweat while reclining on a large heated marble platform. Those wishing to submit their bodies to the most concentrated heat would sit in one of the enclosed areas at each corner of the hot room.

The floor beneath the warm room and the hot room was to be supported above a shallow open space called a hypocaust. Hot gases from the adjacent furnace would travel through this space to flues buried in the walls. An array of small chimneys on the roof could be opened or closed to regulate the flow of these gases, thereby raising or lowering the temperature of the rooms below. Hot water and steam from the boiler above the furnace was to be piped into the hot room.

Hamam of Suha Mehmet Pasa

warm room

heating flue

hot room

to hypocaust

furnace and boiler room

191

During the months it would take to complete both sets of foundations, Agha and his assistants spent much of their time estimating the quantities of the various building materials required, locating adequate sources, and establishing firm and acceptable prices. Only by careful planning early on could they hope to stay within the high but not infinite budget the admiral had set aside or avoid running out of a particular material at any point in the process.

The most important building material was high-quality stone, much of which would come from a large quarry near the western city of Edirne. Gangs of quarrymen first pried great slabs off the cliff face and then divided them into smaller pieces. Stonecutters next chiseled these irregular lumps into rough rectangular blocks that were then loaded on carts for the 140-mile-long journey to Istanbul. Once they reached the site, these blocks would be cut to their final dimensions and dressed by master masons and their apprentices.

1.

Another important building material was brick, much of which came from the nearby brickyard at Haskoy. There groups of men carefully mixed precise quantities of washed sand and clay, which was then carted over to one of the sheds, where skilled craftsmen molded it into bricks of various shapes and sizes. Every available piece of ground was covered by rows of wet bricks drying in the sun. After three days, these same bricks would be baked in one of the large kilns for three more days. Those to be used in the construction of walls were larger and somewhat heavier than those being produced for the domes.

2.

By November, the streets between the site and harbor were often impassable as one cartload of material after another slowly wound its way up the hill. In addition to roughly shaped foundation blocks, which continued to arrive from the quarries of Kadikoy, there were shipments of fine stone from Edirne, long, straight tree trunks from the forests around the Black Sea, and lime from local kilns for making mortar and cement.

3.

4.

In December, traffic throughout the city was considerably hampered by layers of snow and ice. Construction of the foundations came to a complete standstill as below-freezing temperatures made it impossible to mix reliable concrete or mortar. Throughout the winter months work continued in the sheds and workshops as masons prepared thousands of square-cut stone blocks for the walls as well as marble capitals and bases for the tops and bottoms of various columns.

Jewish merchants, whose shops and offices were located along the narrow streets near the harbor, maintained a steady supply of ore from the provinces beyond Edirne. Blacksmiths working all around the city turned this ore into the thousands of connectors that would be needed to strengthen the masonry walls.

In a factory behind one such forge, workers assembled pieces of cut wrought iron into the grilles that would secure the window openings around the lower levels of the prayer hall. Sturdy rods were fastened together using specially made connectors called knots.

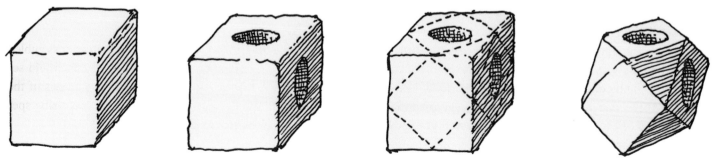

Shaping a knot

It wasn't until early March that work resumed on the foundations. But by that time, Bey had things so well organized that no sooner did a shipment of stone arrive on the site than it was quickly swallowed up by the waiting trenches. By June 24 the foundations were finished. To the admiral's great delight, the future locations of each wall, pier, and column were now plainly visible. He was on hand early one morning for the ceremonial orienting of the mihrab on the foundations of the kibla wall. A ram was sacrificed and its blood was placed at each corner of the prayer hall. To express his gratitude, Suha Mehmet Pasa personally distributed presents to some of the foremen.

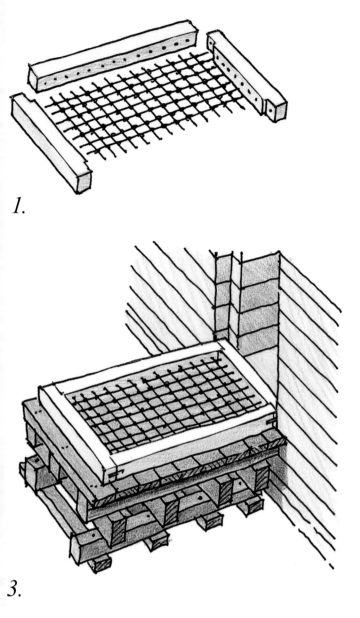

1.

2.

bench

3.

4.

5.

Over the summer, the walls of the prayer hall rose in one continuous ring, climbing steadily toward the base of the great dome. They were faced inside and out with carefully cut stone, which the masons tied together with iron clamps and bars. To strengthen the walls further, vertical rods were inserted to bind each layer of stone to the one above it. The cavity between the inner and outer faces was filled with rubble and cement.

When the walls reached the tops of the window openings, the iron grilles were fixed in place. At the base of each opening, carpenters first erected a sturdy wooden bench upon which a grille and its surrounding stone frame were fitted together. The entire bench was then tipped upward, guiding the completed assembly into place.

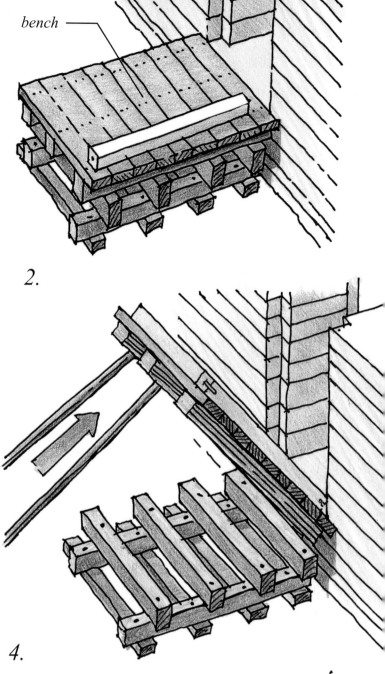

centering

Using a temporary wooden frame called a centering, masons next built an arch over every window and door opening to deflect the weight safely down to the sides. As the walls rose higher and higher, scaffolding was erected along both sides to support work platforms.

By autumn, the seven bays of the portico were beginning to take shape. Since the primary purpose of the portico was to give latecomers to Friday services an appropriate place to pray, Agha had called for two niches to be built into the walls, one on each side of the portal. These would repeat the form and orientation of the mihrab. At one end of the portico, a small door opened onto a stairway leading to the women's gallery. A similar door at the opposite end led to the spiral staircase of the minaret. With its own built-in stairway, most of the minaret could be constructed without scaffolding in spite of its great height.

Four ancient marble columns, discovered by workers digging the foundations of the hamam, were trimmed and set onto newly carved bases to support the high arches of the portico.

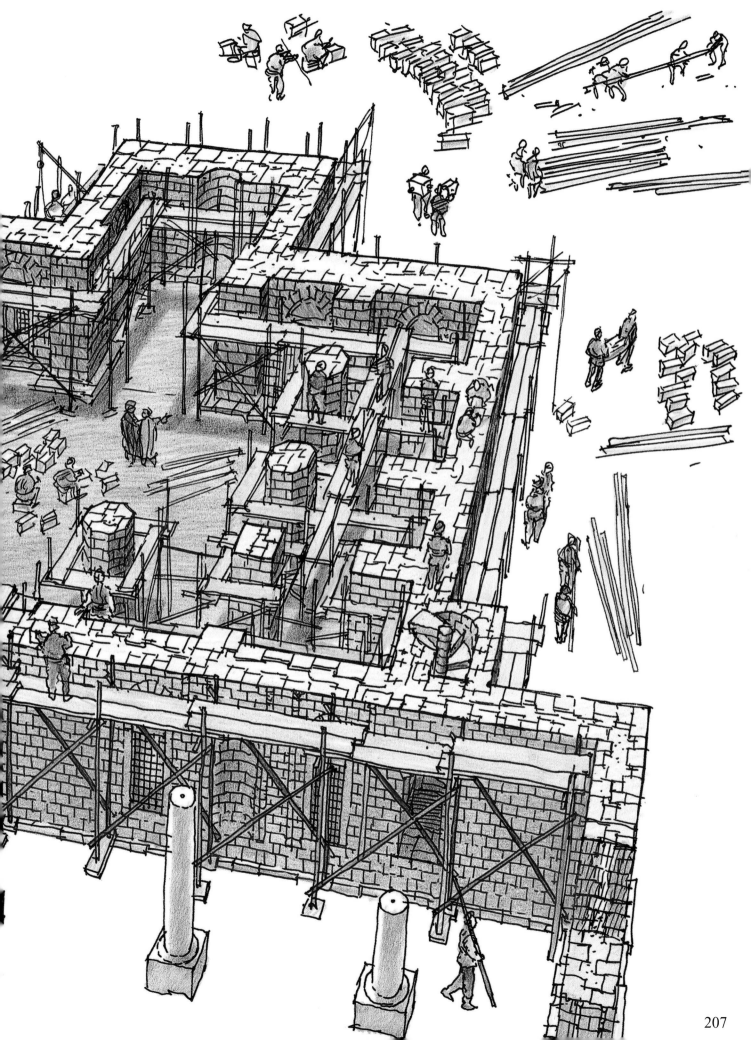

207

A carved marble capital was secured to the top of each column. These capitals were then tied together and to the walls with heavy iron rods above which wooden centerings were inserted for the construction of the arches.

Each bay of the portico would be covered by a small dome. Since each dome had to rest on a continuous circular base, triangular supports called pendentives were built out from each corner of all seven bays. The precise curvature of these pendentives was determined by using a straight wooden pole that could pivot freely from the top of a post at the center of each bay. A nail hammered into the pole at a predetermined distance from the pivot drew an imaginary arc up to which the bricks were laid. As the angle of the pole grew steeper, each successive course of bricks had to be extended a littler farther into the space to meet the arc.

The pole was also used to establish and maintain the curvature of each dome. Unlike the bricks of the pendentives, which were laid flat, those of the domes were set at an angle. The slant of the pole helped to establish the correct slope of each brick.

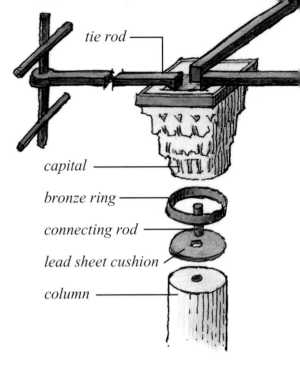

tie rod

capital

bronze ring

connecting rod

lead sheet cushion

column

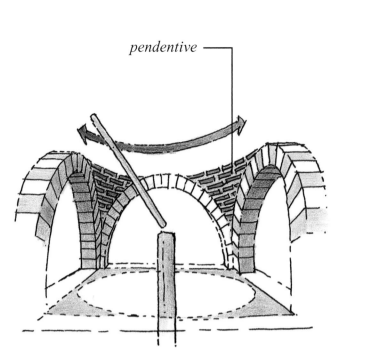

pendentive

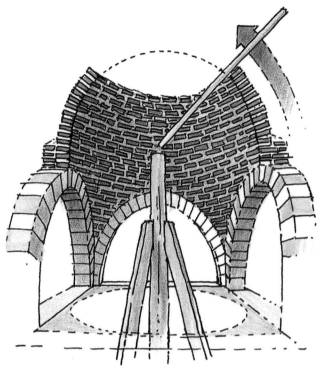

Lead sheets that would eventually cover each dome were made in a number of different workshops around the city. The master sheet maker first sprinkled a little sand over the surface of his specially built masonry bench while an assistant stirred the molten lead. When all was ready, the assistant ladled a predetermined amount into a tray at one end of the bench. The tray was then upended, spilling out its silvery contents. With a few precise movements of his board, the master carefully spread the lead to achieve a uniform thickness before it solidified. The finished sheet was still hot as it was peeled from the bench.

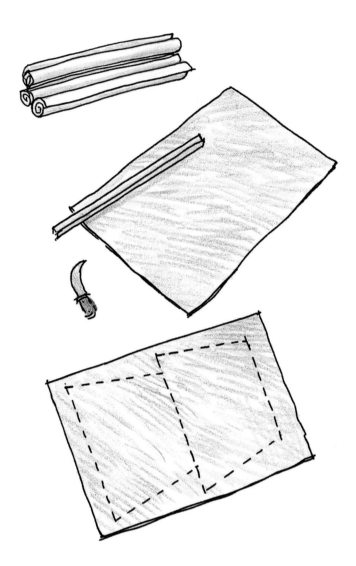

Each dome was first covered with a layer of specially prepared mud. Once hardened, this coating not only helped protect the bricks but also provided an ideal base for the lead sheets. Using a string attached to the top of the dome, the roofers scratched lines on the mud to determine the exact shape of each sheet. Beginning around the base of the dome, each sheet was nailed into place and their sides bent upward. This process was repeated until the entire dome was covered. Once all the sheets were in place, each vertical row of adjacent edges was rolled into a single seam. The cluster of seams that came together at the crest of the dome was made watertight and held in place first with a round lead collar and then with a heavy stone cap.

By December 25, the tops of most of the piers and walls stood temporarily tied together by a network of wooden centerings over which the supporting arches for the semi-domes would soon be assembled.

While the prayer hall grew steadily within its man-made forest of scaffolding, the slender minaret, still completely unencumbered by such trappings, was beginning to pull away. Its builders—a group of highly skilled workers who

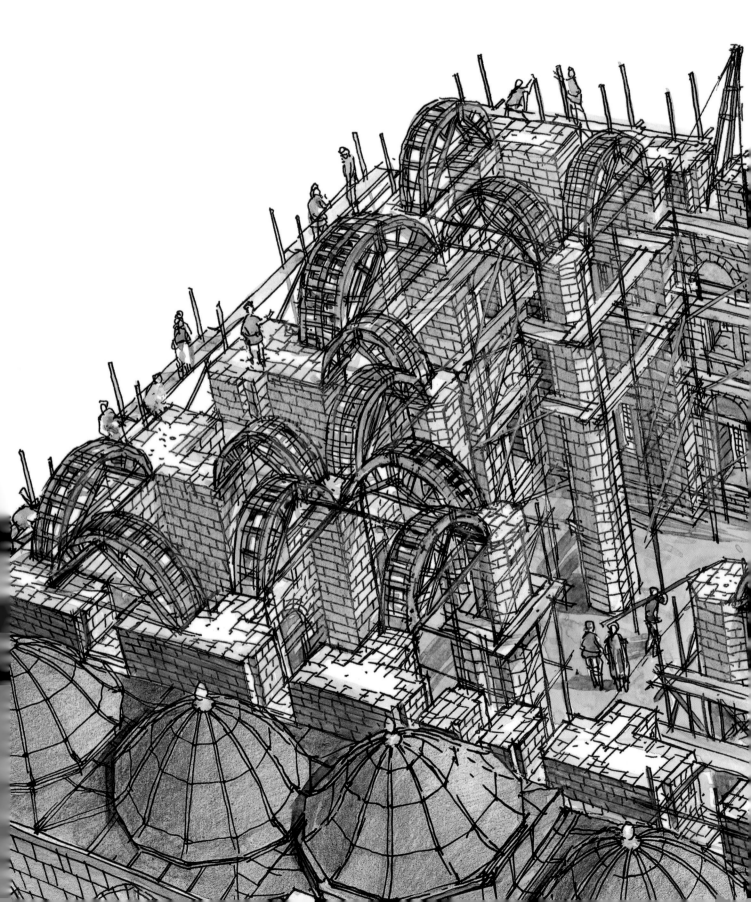

specialized in such construction and traveled together from one site to another—took great care in fitting and clamping one stone to the next. The spiral staircase itself was constructed of flat, wedge-shaped steps piled one on top of the other. The narrow end of each wedge was cut into a cylindrical shape. As the staircase rose, these stacked cylinders created a continuous central core. The wide end of each step was set into the wall, further strengthening the tower.

The first months of 1598 were unusually mild, allowing work to proceed without interruption. By March, the simpler, mostly solid walls of the hamam were almost ready to receive their domes. Agha had designed a high arch into each corner of the cold room. This increased the number of pendentives that would be required, but more important, it reduced their size and weight. Each arch was buttressed by a small semidome.

The large domes of the cold and hot rooms were built using complete hemispherical wooden forms over which the bricks could be laid quickly and easily. The smaller domes and semidomes were built using the pole method.

By May, the bases for the semidomes of the prayer hall were complete. For additional stability, each was reinforced with a heavy iron tie rod. Various cranes and hoists were used to raise centerings and building materials to the tops of the walls in preparation for the building of the eight large arches that would eventually support the high dome. Since the minaret provided the best view of all that was going on, Akif Agha and Huseyin Bey often passed each other on the stairway. Occasionally His Excellency himself would make the long climb.

217

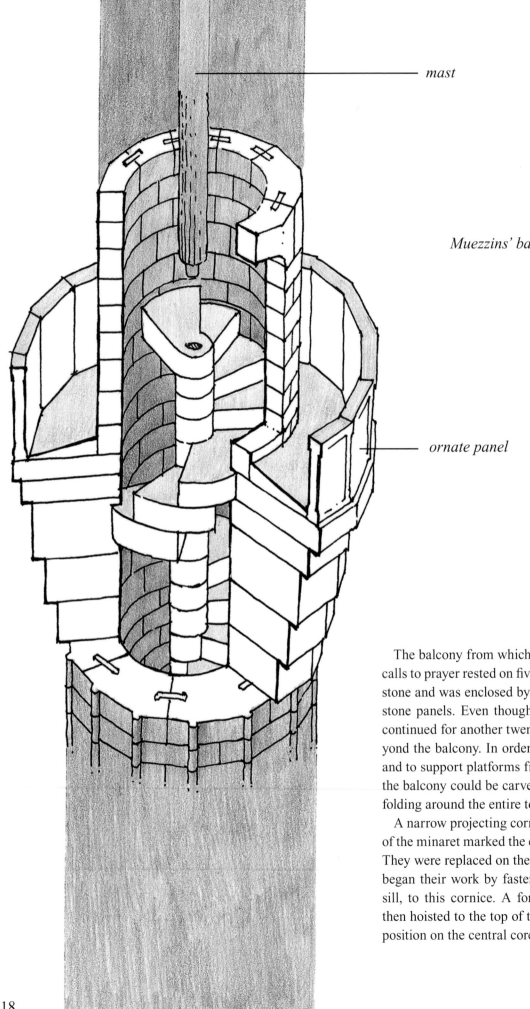

mast

Muezzins' balcony

ornate panel

The balcony from which the muezzins would issue their calls to prayer rested on five gradually widening courses of stone and was enclosed by a wall of ornately carved limestone panels. Even though the exterior wall of the tower continued for another twenty feet, only four steps rose beyond the balcony. In order to complete the minaret safely and to support platforms from which the stonework below the balcony could be carved, carpenters now erected scaffolding around the entire tower.

A narrow projecting cornice crowning the upper portion of the minaret marked the end of the masons' contribution. They were replaced on the scaffolding by the roofers, who began their work by fastening a narrow wooden base, or sill, to this cornice. A forty-foot-long wooden mast was then hoisted to the top of the scaffolding and lowered into position on the central core.

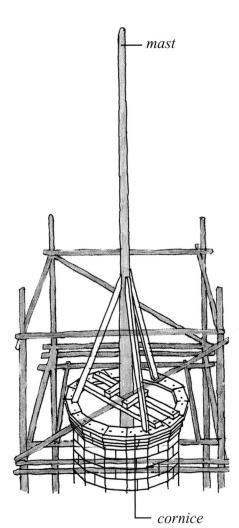

mast

cornice

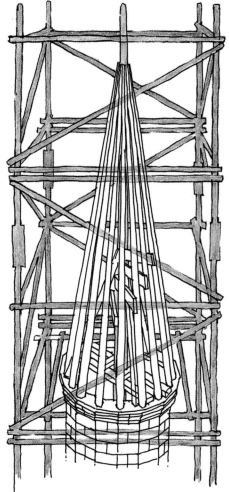

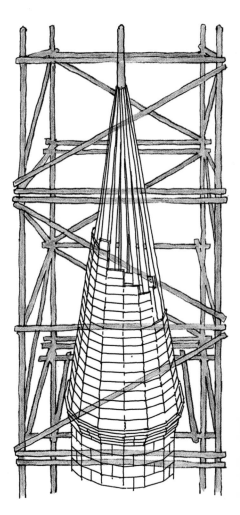

alem

The ring of long poles that would give the roof its distinct shape was installed next, followed by a layer of cladding boards and sheets of insulating felt—since mud would never have worked at such an angle. Once sheathed in lead, the graceful silver-gray cone was almost finished.

It was a clear June day when the admiral, accompanied by an officer from Queen Elizabeth's visiting fleet, stood on the muezzins' balcony. They had to come to watch the pieces of the copper alem—a specially constructed finial—being stacked over the exposed tip of the mast. Before beginning their descent, the old Ottoman sailor challenged his British colleague to join him out on the scaffolding for a closer look at the intricate stalactite carving beneath the balcony.

With construction of the prayer hall well in hand, Bey was able to assign more workers to the courtyard. This enclosed, arcaded space had three entrances, one near each end of the portico and a third—slightly larger—on the kibla. The marble columns that would support the colonnade had all been shipped from Marmara Island, which was located in the sea south of the city. As the surrounding stone walls grew, window openings were built into each bay to provide pleasant views of the trees and flowers that would eventually occupy the space between the courtyard and the precinct wall. The foundations for the sadirvan and the cistern within it were dug, and a pipe was laid from the nearest water tower. A second water pipe extended to the toilets at the northwest corner of the precinct. A covered channel would carry the waste and overflow out into the street drains.

By the end of September 1598, the main arches and their pendentives were finished. Small false domes were still being completed above the weight towers that now stood like sentries at each corner of the great octagon.

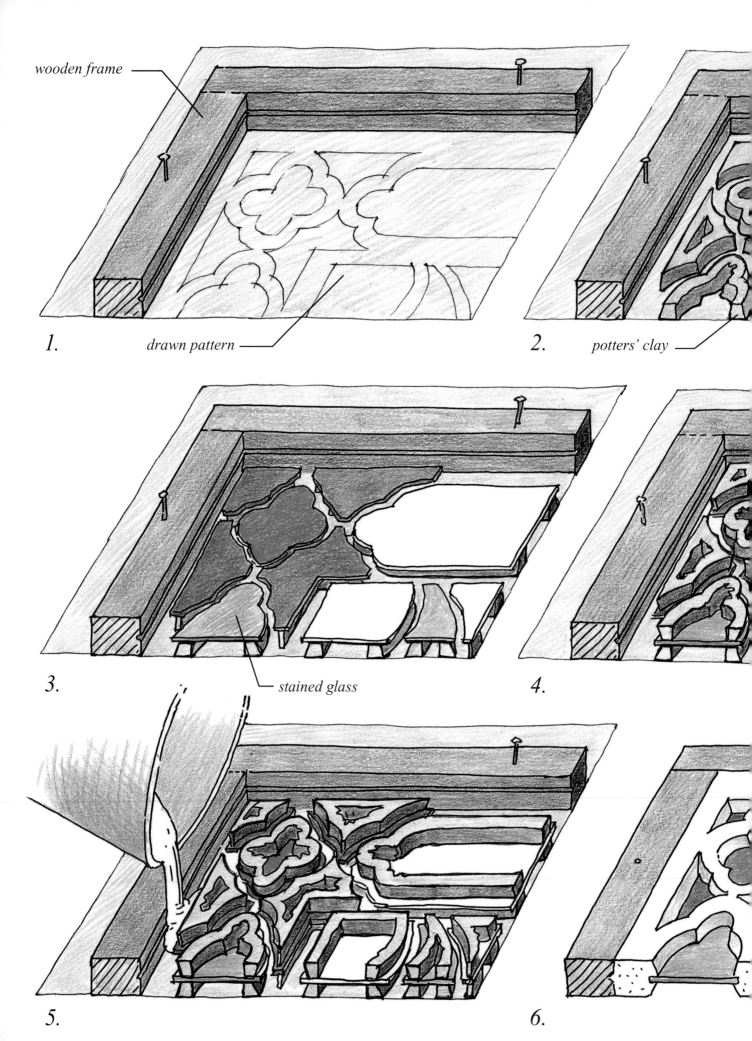

1. wooden frame

drawn pattern

2. potters' clay

3. stained glass

4.

5.

6.

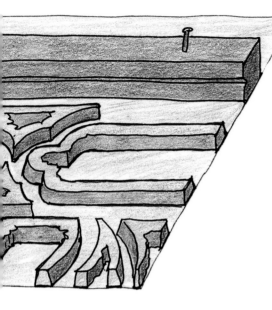

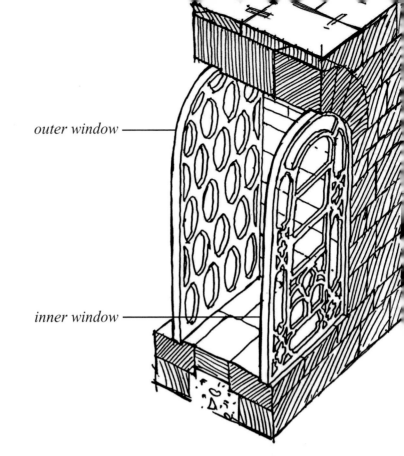

outer window ——

inner window ——

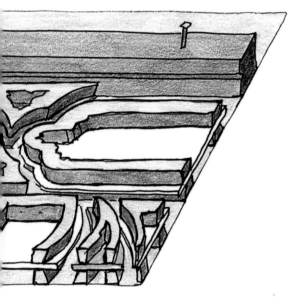

plaster ——

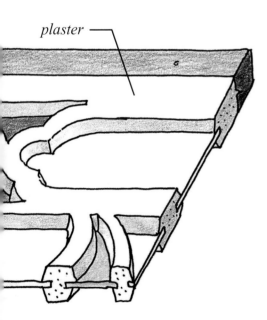

Since all the openings above the first and second levels of the prayer hall were for light alone and not ventilation, they were fitted with pairs of fixed windows. The outer windows contained only clear glass. Those on the inside were made of richly colored (and considerably more expensive) Venetian glass.

The pattern for each window was first drawn on paper and then laid out on the window maker's bench. A wooden frame was then lightly nailed around the pattern. Thin strips of potters' clay were placed inside the frame precisely following the drawn lines. Carefully cut pieces of glass were then set on top of the clay, after which a second layer of clay strips was added. Finally, a thin mixture of plaster of Paris was poured into the cavities between the clay strips to create the tracery that holds the glass in place. Once the plaster had set to the master's satisfaction, the frame was lifted off the bench and the clay carefully scraped out. The outer windows were made the same way, but the pieces of clear glass were either round or half round, and a much more durable, cementlike mixture was used.

The window openings around the lower levels provided both light and ventilation. No glass was used in these openings, only wooden shutters hinged behind the iron grilles.

By the middle of October, the hamam was ready for its first patrons. Natural light entered the cold room through a combination of stained-glass windows set into the walls and several smaller windows contained in the cupola on top of the dome. In order to contain the heat in the hot room, no windows had been inserted into the walls. The only natural light entering this space came through small clear glass bubbles set into the dome. With the furnace fired up and the appropriate temperature reached, the admiral led his entourage into the hamam for its inaugural bath. After pronouncing the experience most satisfactory, he once again ordered that presents be distributed to the builders. Until the rest of the admiral's kulliye was finished, the baths were to serve only men. Eventually, however, an alternating schedule would be established permitting its use by both men and women.

Eight months later, in spite of the normal winter inter-
ruptions, presents were once again being distributed by a
grateful patron—this time to celebrate the completion of
the semidomes. From the masonry ring upon which the
high dome itself would soon rise, Agha directed the admiral's attention to the foundation work already under way
for both the adjacent medrese and the imaret just across
the road.

The basic layout of both the medrese and the imaret was quite similar—rows of dome-covered rooms surrounding large open courtyards. Since most of the teaching at the school would take place either in the prayer hall or, weather permitting, outside, all but one of the rooms in the medrese were dormitories. The exception was the dershane, a large lecture hall that would also house His Excellency's fine collection of books.

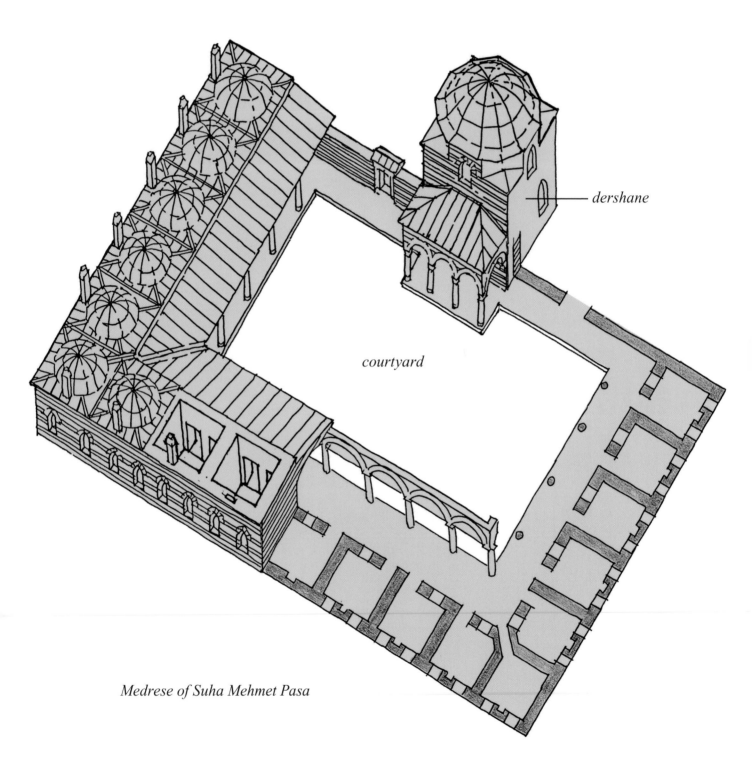

dershane

courtyard

Medrese of Suha Mehmet Pasa

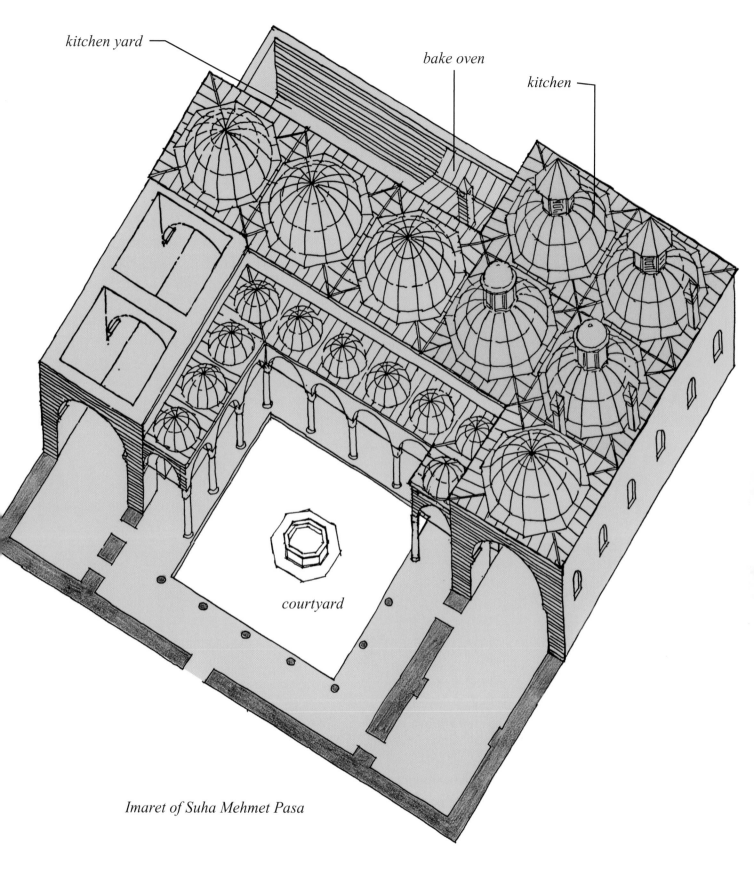

kitchen yard

bake oven

kitchen

courtyard

Imaret of Suha Mehmet Pasa

While the mosque would join the hearts and minds of the faithful through their devotion to God, the imaret would link the community within the kulliye to the community outside through their stomachs. All the rooms leading off the courtyard were dining rooms in which the staff and students of the complex would be fed, along with the poor and needy of the neighborhood. At the rear of the building, farthest away from the mosque, Agha had placed the large kitchen, complete with its own bakery.

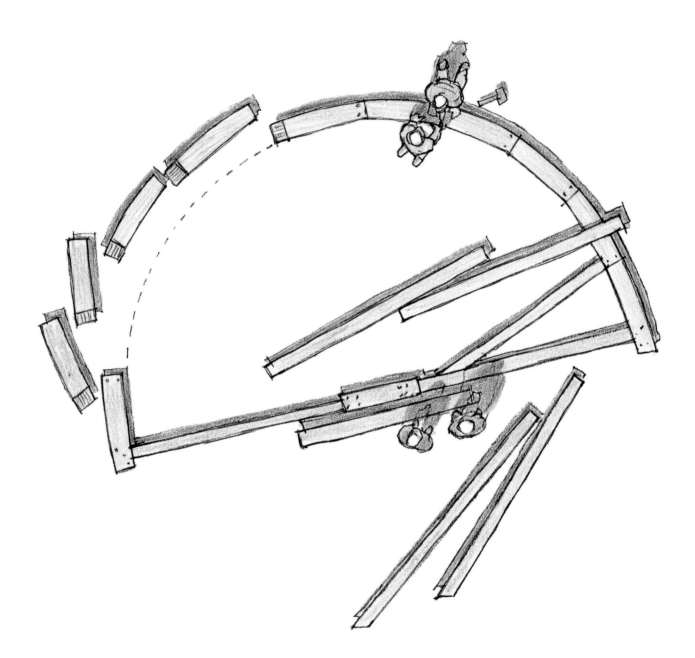

High above the prayer hall, Agha employed a third method for determining the shape and proportion of the great dome. Rather than using a single pole, which might prove less reliable at this scale, or having to build and support a heavy wooden form high up in the scaffolding, he instructed his carpenters to create a flat semicircular arch that would be rigid enough to maintain its shape and yet light enough to rotate easily on a fixed iron support. The form was first assembled on the ground and checked for accuracy. It was then taken apart and hoisted piece by piece to the top of the central scaffolding, where it was carefully reassembled and set onto its pivot.

While the thickness of the upper half of the dome would be established by the dimensions of the bricks used in its construction, the base would have to be made considerably wider. Not only did it have to resist the outward-pushing forces within the dome, but it also had to compensate for weight sacrificed to window openings. An interconnected ring of heavy iron bars was embedded near the tops of these windows to provide additional strength.

Bricklayers working at both ends of the wooden form carefully set each brick on a thick bed of mortar. To prevent the bricks from slipping, small wedges of brick were inserted between them. When a complete ring of bricks was in place and its mortar had sufficiently hardened, the next course could be safely built on top of it.

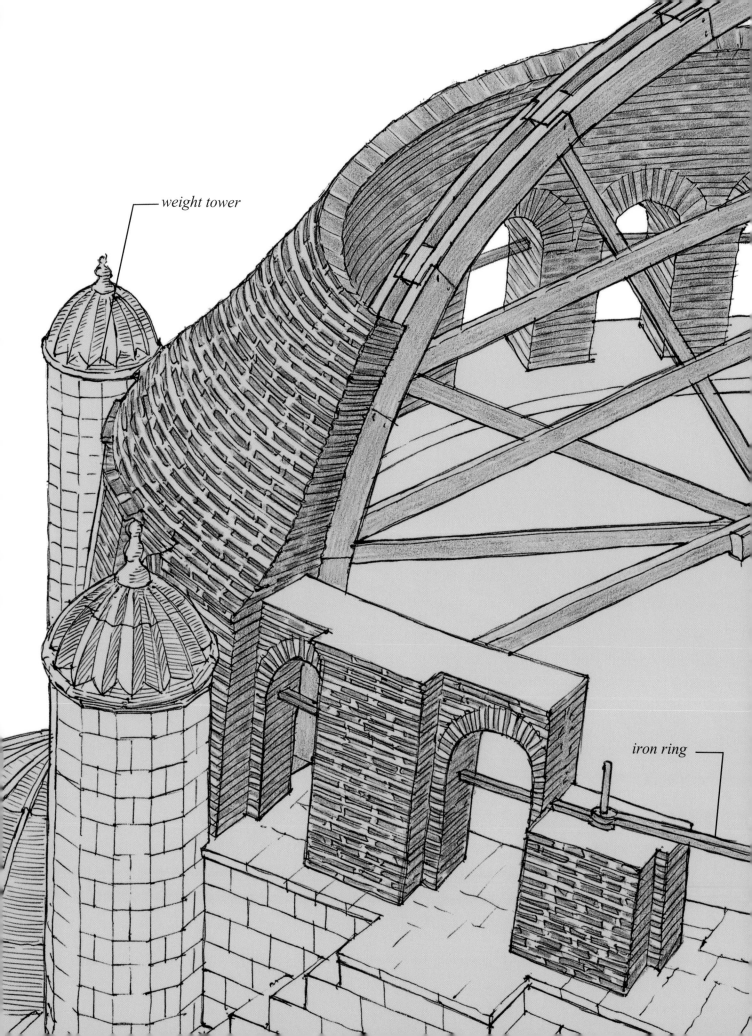

weight tower

iron ring

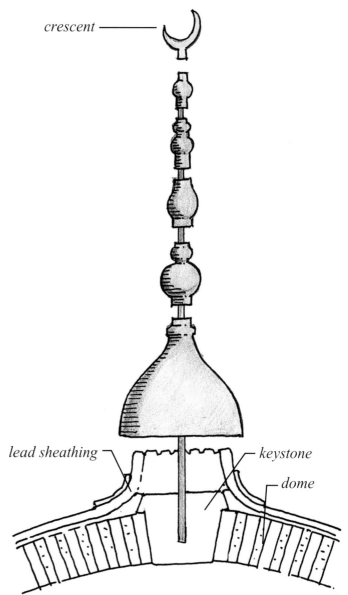

crescent

lead sheathing

keystone

dome

bronze alem

Over the following months, the circle of sky at the top of the dome continued to shrink. The last bit of light was finally snuffed out with the insertion of the keystone. By early spring, the entire hemisphere stood sheathed and waiting for the ceremony accompanying the installation of its bronze alem. There was great excitement as each piece was slipped carefully over the iron rod set into the keystone.

Cheers rose from every corner of the site when the gilded crescent was finally added. This time the admiral had brought several of his sons with him to help distribute presents to the workers.

Although it would be several more months before the mosque was completely finished and even longer before the entire complex was operating, employees of the foundation's various programs, including those who would help maintain the buildings, had already been hired. Upon the recommendation of the ulema, a body of the most respected scholars of the Koran, the admiral had engaged a distinguished imam to lead the prayers and serve as one of the teachers in the medrese. Included among the scores of additional employees were more teachers, muezzins, clerks, caretakers, gardeners, lamplighters, and even a librarian. With its staff now assembled, the foundation's official deed was finally recorded on April 3, 1600.

Turbe of Suha Mehmet Pasa

After the ceremony, the admiral paid a brief visit to the site of his turbe, the foundations of which were already rising on the kibla behind the prayer hall. In accordance with his client's wishes, Agha had designed an octagonal building of great simplicity.

Now that the prayer hall was completely sealed against the elements, full attention could be given to the adornment of its interior surfaces. By tradition, all the decoration was to be derived from three sources—the words of the Koran, natural vegetation, and geometric patterns.

Much of this decoration was painted and baked onto ceramic tiles. The rest would either be painted on or carved into plaster, stone, or wood. Akif Agha gave instructions about the general placement of decoration and the materials to be used, as well as the choices of text to be included. He left such decisions as specific patterns, shapes, and colors to the experienced craftsmen who would carry out the work.

Once the size and shape of a calligraphic panel had been determined, the selected text was written full size in Arabic. The finished sheets of paper were then passed along to an artisan who carefully traced the outline of each stroke with a row of pinholes. Coal dust pressed through the pinholes would leave a precise outline to guide each craftsman in his work.

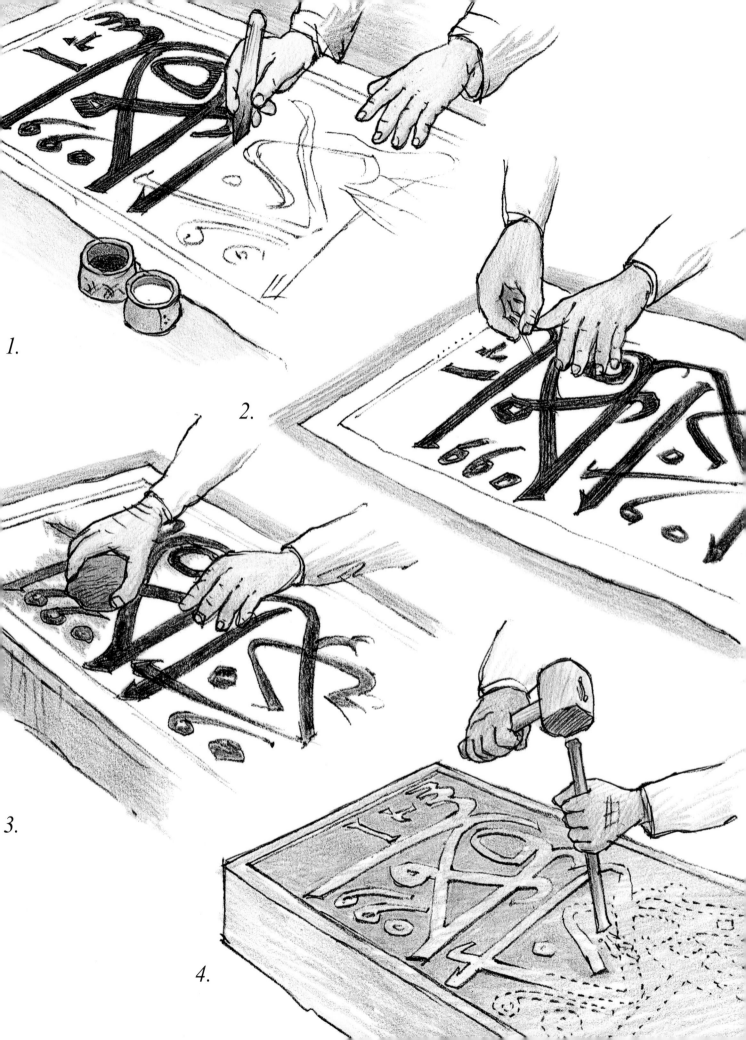

1.

2.

3.

4.

Most of the ceramic tiles were imported from the famous kilns of Iznik in Anatolia. In addition to the blue and white calligraphic panels, their craftsmen also created richly colored tiles based on the lines and shapes of various flowers and vines.

In the painted decoration of the central dome, floral designs were combined with text. To underscore the significance of the words, a layer of glue was applied to each letter and then painstakingly covered with gold dust.

Elsewhere in the prayer hall, a variety of geometric patterns was being completed, from the capitals of the columns and piers, to the stone railings running along the galleries, to the ceilings beneath them.

Artisans in another part of the city were putting the final touches on pieces of the minber. Elaborate geometric patterns had been fashioned from hundreds of small pieces of wood while areas of carved decoration filled the remaining space.

At another workshop, a pattern had been drawn on the floor to serve as a guide for the fabrication of the great chandelier that would eventually hang over the center of the prayer hall. This large iron frame would support a constellation of oil lamps above the heads of the worshipers.

Since the mihrab was the primary focus of attention during prayer, it and the wall around it naturally received the greatest concentration of decoration. The marble-lined mihrab was recessed between two false columns and be-low a gilded stone pediment. The stalactite carvings with which the mihrab culminated were also covered in gold. A collection of the finest floral and calligraphic tiles filled the entire space up to and surrounding the three stained-glass windows, which appeared to float below the semidome.

When the prayer hall was at last free of scaffolding, the ground was compacted, covered with a bed of cement, and finished with a layer of tiles.

On July 27, 1600, almost three years after the ceremonial placement of the mihrab, the completed mosque was dedicated. Joining the admiral and his family were representatives of the court, the military, and the ulema. Also in attendance were members of the various guilds that had worked on the buildings, including Huseyin Bey and all nine of his sons, several of Akif Agha's assistants from the office of the Court Architect, and assorted members of the local community.

Following ablutions, the entire entourage moved from the sadirvan to the portico, where they removed their shoes. As the admiral's wives and daughters turned toward the stairwell leading to the women's gallery, Suha Mehmet Pasa led the men through the main portal and into the prayer hall.

Bathed in light filtering through countless pieces of colored glass, they slowly moved across the sea of carpets that covered the floor. As the assembled placed their prayer mats side by side and end to end, their eyes were drawn upward past the sparkling tiles and radiant gilding, past the deeply cut panels of stalactite carving, to Agha's great dome, which seemed to float weightlessly above them. Most were still admiring their surroundings as Suha Mehmet Pasa climbed the steps of the minber to give his speech. After thanking all those who had, with God's help, transformed his vision into reality, the proud yet humbled admiral returned to his place facing the kibla wall. Then as the imam lead the congregation in prayer, the splendor of the architecture in which they were gathered temporarily faded. Each worshiper now entered a more intimate space —a space defined completely by the five positions of prayer within the borders of his own prayer mat.

While the decorators had been at work inside the prayer hall, the adjacent medrese had been completed. Each of its simply finished rooms, which now housed up to three students, had its own fireplace, pair of windows, and recessed shelves for a few personal belongings.

257

The imaret, on the other hand, had proven to be more of a challenge. Due to the slope of the site and the instability of the soil, it had been necessary first to construct a large vaulted basement under almost half of the building. It wasn't until October 15, 1600, that Agha and Bey finally toured the finished structure. In the all-important kitchen, they found the staff of the imaret busily preparing the midday meal. Smoke from beneath great cauldrons of simmering soup rose toward the carefully placed vents that rested on two of the four domes. The other two had been capped by window-filled cupolas to admit more light into the space. As workers scurried back and forth with food for the tables and fuel for the fires, the smell of freshly baked bread, bubbling soup, and rich spices filled the air.

On his way back to the office, a well-fed Akif Agha walked past the cesme, which he had set into the precinct wall facing the imaret. From the moment the first cool water had flowed into the stone basin, it had become one of the most popular gathering places in the neighborhood—a sight that gave the architect particular pleasure.

Two weeks later, as Agha was overseeing the installation of the doors to the recently completed turbe, word reached him that the admiral had been stricken—apparently as he reached for figs in his cherished garden—and had departed this earth for the rewards of an even greater paradise. The admiral's remains were soon resting in the ground beneath his empty cloth-draped coffin.

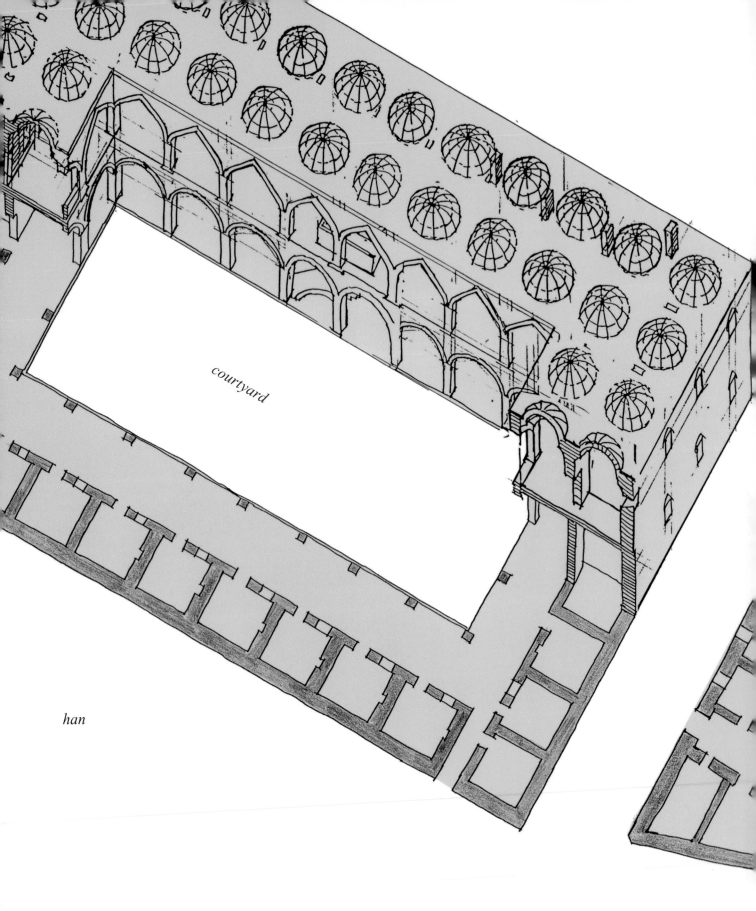

courtyard

han

Han and caravanserai of Suha Mehmet Pasa

With his patron's passing, Akif Agha had naturally assumed that his work on the old man's behalf was complete. Several months after Suha Mehmet Pasa's death, however, he was informed that the admiral's favorite wife, who was also one of the sultan's many cousins, wished to ensure her late husband's legacy by adding a han and a caravanserai to the kulliye. Over the years these two buildings would generate income to help support the activities of the foundation.

The ground floor of the han would be rented out to local businessmen and artisans. The second level would offer accommodations to out-of town guests and bachelors. The second level of the caravanserai would also offer accommodations, but this time to caravan drivers. Their beasts were to be housed in a large vaulted stable below. Whereas the han was placed next to the imaret, Agha located the caravanserai farther from the prayer hall and along a busy street close to the harbor. The rooms of both buildings were once again laid out around courtyards. Not only would this arrangement provide a secure outdoor gathering place, but it would ensure that plenty of light and air reached all of the surrounding rooms.

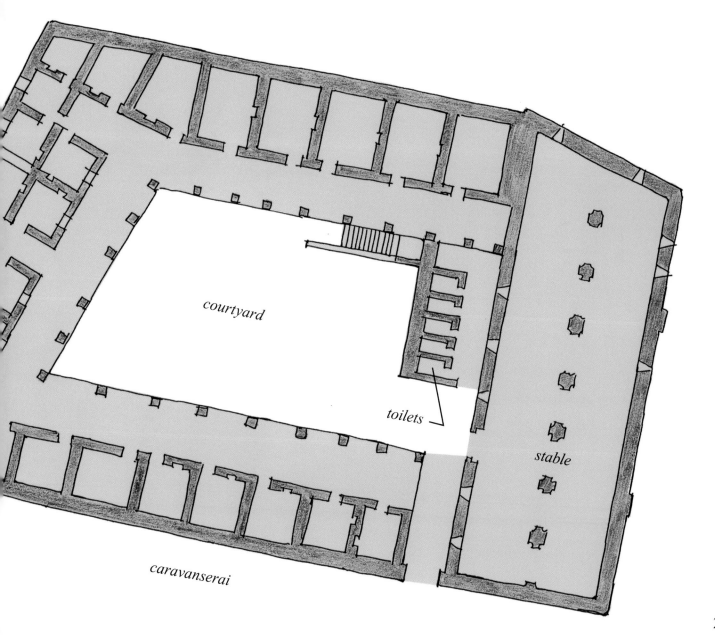

courtyard

toilets

stable

caravanserai

Leaving the project in Bey's reliable hands, Akif Agha spent most of the next two years away from the city. Part of that time was spent participating in the hajj, the great pilgrimage to Mecca that all able-bodied Muslims were expected to make. The remainder was spent either overseeing repairs to the extensive supply system that brought water to Istanbul or working on commissions for several of the sultan's most important ministers and viziers.

By the time Agha settled back into city life, the han and the caravanserai were not only finished but flourishing. The surrounding streets were once again clogged with carts. Though now instead of stone and scaffolding they were laden with baskets of fruit, bundles of flowers and precious woods, bolts of richly colored fabric, and sacks of fragrant spices. Even the narrow side streets were filled with activity. Tinsmiths and cloth merchants displayed their wares outside the entrances to their shops. Hawkers and performers vied for customers. Glasses of tea were filled and sold from urns carried on the backs of a handful of wandering vendors. Children ran among soldiers and holy men; travelers from distant cities mixed with locals. Several times a day, the cacophony of the streets was tempered by the periodic call to prayer from the muezzins' balcony.

When completed, the kulliye of Suha Mehmet Pasa officially comprised seven buildings, but unofficially it had spawned hundreds more. New houses, shops, workshops, factories, warehouses, and countless large and small gardens now filled the surrounding plots of land where charred timber and burned bricks had once been piled. Though memories of the great fire undoubtedly lingered, all the ashes had long ago become part of the soil upon which new life was now thriving.

GLOSSARY

AISLE The part of a church that runs parallel to the main areas—nave, choir, and transept—and is separated from them by an arcade.

ALEM The finial placed on top of the dome or minaret of a mosque.

APSE The semi-circular or polygonal end of a church, usually the east end.

ARCADE The row of piers and arches that separate the main spaces of the cathedral from the aisles.

ARROW LOOP A narrow vertical slit cut into a wall through which arrows could be fired from the inside.

BATTER The angled or sloping base of all the walls and towers of a castle along their exterior surface.

BATTLEMENT A narrow wall built of alternating high and low sections along the outer edge of the castle wall walk to protect the soldiers against attack.

BUTTRESS A large stone pier built against or connected to a wall to provide extra strength.

CAPITAL The form, usually of stone, that supplies the visual transition between the top of a column and whatever the column supports.

CARAVANSERAI An overnight stopping place for caravans that provided safe accommodation for both the drivers and the animals.

CATHEDRAL A church of any size that contains the cathedra, or bishop's chair.

CENTERING The temporary timber framework that supports the stones of an arch until the mortar between them has set.

CESME A public drinking fountain.

CESSPIT The opening in a castle wall from which the waste from one or more garderobes was collected.

CHOIR The section of the church east of the transept that is sometimes raised above the level of the nave. It is called the choir because traditionally this is where the choir stands to sing during the service.

CISTERN A tank for storing water.

CLERESTORY The topmost part of the church building, the windows of which illuminate the central portion of the interior space.

CORBEL A projecting block of stone built into a wall during construction.

CRENELATION Battlement.

CROWN The highest part of the arch, where the keystone is located.

CRYPT A lower level of a cathedral, usually below ground, that is used for burial or as a chapel.

CUPOLA A small domed structure crowning a larger dome or roof and often filled with windows.

DAUB A mud or clay mixture applied over wattle to strengthen and seal it.

DOME An arched ceiling of even curvature built on a circular base.

DRAWBRIDGE   A heavy timber platform built to span a moat between a castle's gatehouse and surrounding land. The drawbridge could be raised to block the entrance.

DUNGEON   The jail, usually found in one of the towers of a castle.

EMBRASURE   The low segment of the alternating high and low segments of a castle battlement.

FALSE DOME   A structure with the form of a dome on the outside but supported on the inside with wood or masonry.

FINIAL   A slender vertical piece of stone used to decorate the tops of the merlons.

FORGE   Both the furnace in which metal is heated to a high temperature and the workshop in which heated metal is hammered into various shapes.

FOUNDATION   The underground construction required to distribute the weight of a wall and to prevent its uneven settlement.

FLYING BUTTRESS   In a cathedral, a stone arch that carries the outward forces of the vault to the buttress.

GARDEROBE   A small latrine or toilet either built into the thickness of a castle wall or projected out from it.

GATEHOUSE   The complex of towers and barriers built to protect each entrance through a castle or town wall.

GREAT HALL   The building in the inner ward of a castle that housed the main meeting and dining area for the castle's residents.

HALF-TIMBER   The most common form of medieval construction in which walls were made of a wooden framework filled with wattle and daub.

HAMAM   A public bathhouse containing cold, warm, and hot rooms.

HAN   A two-story building in which space could be rented for conducting business and for accommodation.

HOARDING   A temporary wooden balcony suspended from the tops of castle walls and towers before a battle, from which missiles and arrows could be dropped and fired accurately toward the bases of the walls.

HURDLE   A movable work platform made of woven twigs.

IMAM   The man who leads a mosque's congregation in prayer.

IMARET   Soup kitchen and public dining room.

INNER CURTAIN   The high castle wall that surrounds the inner ward.

INNER WARD   The open area in the center of a castle.

KAABA   The great shrine in Mecca that all Muslims face when praying.

KEYSTONE   The central locking stone at the top of an arch.

KIBLA   The direction of Mecca.

KIBLA WALL   The front wall of a prayer hall, always located perpendicular to the kibla, facing Mecca.

KORAN   The sacred text of Islam.

KULLIYE   The complex buildings associated with a mosque and its charitable foundation.

LAGGING Temporary wooden frames used in the contruction of vaulting.

MECCA The birthplace of the prophet Muhammad.

MEDRESE A college for Muslim education.

MERLON The high segment of the alternating high and low segments of a castle's battlement.

MIHRAB The niche in the center of a mosque's kibla wall indicating the direction of Mecca, from in front of which the imam leads the prayers.

MINARET The tower from which Muslims are called to prayer five times a day.

MINBER The high, stepped pulpit used for sermons at Friday services at a mosque.

MOAT A deep trench dug around a castle to prevent access from the surrounding land. It could either be left dry or filled with water.

MORTAR A mixture of sand, water, and lime used to bind stones together permanently.

MORTICE AND TENON A method of fastening one piece of wood to another. A mortice, or hole, is cut into one piece of wood while a tenon, or projection, the same size as the hole is whittled out of the other piece. The tenon is then tapped into the mortice and the two are locked together with an oak peg.

MUEZZIN A cantor who calls the faithful to prayer from the minaret of a mosque.

MULLION The narrow upright stone pier used to divide the panels of glass in a window.

NAVE The central area of a church where the congregation usually stands.

OUTER CURTAIN The wall that encloses the outer ward of a castle.

OUTER WARD The area around the outside of and adjacent to a castle's inner curtain.

PALISADE A sturdy wooden fence usually built to enclose a site until a permanent stone wall can be constructed.

PENDENTIVE A concave support built out from a corner to help form a circular base for the dome above.

PIER The pillar or column that supports an arch.

PORTCULLIS A heavy timber grille that could be raised or lowered between the towers of each castle gatehouse to open or close the passage.

PORTICO A high covered porch that marks the entryway to a prayer hall.

POSTERN GATE A side or less important gate into a castle.

PUTLOG HOLE A hole intentionally left in the surface of a wall for the insertion of a horizontal pole.

RIB The stone arch that supports and strengthens the vault of a cathedral.

RUBBLE A random mixture of rocks and mortar.

SADIRVAN A fountain associated with a mosque and usually located in the center of the courtyard. It contains a cistern in which water is stored for ablutions—the ritual washing of the hands and feet or entire body.

SCAFFOLDING   The temporary wooden framework built next to a wall to support both workers and materials.

SEMIDOME   A half dome.

SIEGE   The military tactic that involves the surrounding and isolation of a castle, town, or army by another army until the trapped forces are starved into surrender.

STALACTITE   A style of ornate ceiling decoration in Islamic architecture in which rows of ornamentation appear to be supported upon one another.

STEWARD   The man responsible for running the day-to-day affairs of the castle in the absence of the lord.

SULTAN   The supreme ruler of a Muslim country, head of the Ottoman Empire.

TEMPLATE   The full-size wooden patter used by the stonecutter when he has to cut many pieces of stone the same size and shape.

TRACERY   The decorative carved stonework of a medieval church window.

TRANSEPT   In a Latin cross plan as at Chutreaux, the section that crosses the nave, usually separating the nave and the choir.

TRIFORIUM   The arcaded story between the nave arcade and the clerestory.

TRUSS   A triangular wooden frame. The roof frame is constructed of a series of trusses fastened together.

TURBE   Tomb.

TYMPANUM   The sculptural area enclosed by the arch above the doors of a cathedral.

ULEMA   The council of the most learned Koran scholars.

VAULT   The form of construction, usually of brick or stone, that is based on the shape of the arch. Used for the most part as a ceiling or roof.

VOUSSOIRS   Blocks of stone cut in wedge shapes to form an arch.

WALL WALK   The area along the tops of the castle walls from which soldiers defended both castle and town.

WATCH TURRET   A small tower rising above and resting on one of the main towers, usually used as a lookout point.

WATTLE   A mat of woven sticks and weeds.

WINDLASS   A machine for hoisting or hauling. In the Middle Ages this consisted of a horizontal wooden barrel with a long rope fastened to it. The barrel was supported at both ends. When it was turned the rope would gradually be wound up around it.